Husband Consultant

Colin Diyen

Langaa Research & Publishing CIG
Mankon, Bamenda

Publisher:
Langaa RPCIG
Langaa Research & Publishing Common Initiative Group
P.O. Box 902 Mankon
Bamenda
North West Region
Cameroon
Langaagrp@gmail.com
www.langaa-rpcig.net

Distributed in and outside N. America by African Books Collective
orders@africanbookscollective.com
www.africanbookcollective.com

ISBN: 9956-717-89-4

DISCLAIMER
All views expressed in this publication are those of the author and do not
necessarily reflect the views of Langaa RPCIG.

Dedication

To my best friends of blessed memory:

Isidore Irvine Diyen, the best Cameroonian I ever knew;

Bah Maya Azah, a very interesting Cameroonian, whose company I enjoyed thoroughly;

And

P.G. Wodehouse, the greatest British humorist of modern times.

Table of Content

Introduction

Many young blokes get confused when it comes to handling women, especially wives. I am saying this because chaps keep prodding at my sides to extract information on simple approaches concerning the handling of females, a thing that even the village fool should be able to do without much of an effort. Tough looking eggs that appear to be capable of chewing glass without even wincing, or of smashing iron blocks into pulp with bare fists, come whimpering and complaining about being rough handled by their women, whereas it would have taken only a drop of good reasoning for theses females to be placed under full control. That is how I found myself transformed from a small hardworking man and father into a superman, who before you say 'boo' can transform henpecked blokes into mature self confident husbands. Were it not for the fact that I could attract tax officers to my humble home, I would have put up one of those elaborate signboards, with the legend 'Husband consultant; handle your spouse with confidence and get all the respect you deserve.' Harried husbands would flow in and fill my pockets with cash the way women in Africa do with quack pastors and medicine men. But then there is always the danger of angry wives rushing in bent on mayhem, when ever I succeeded in transforming their husbands into real men. However, 'always stand by your fellow man' is my motto, so I cannot let my male chums down.

I am not one of those female haters though. What can a man do without a woman by his side? They spice life somehow. Women are like that type of pain that you enjoy as it hurts. You could equally liken them to pepper, a hot spice that many Africans enjoy in their meals despite its sharp burning taste that even makes you perspire uncomfortably.

There are other attributes to a woman which most men do not realize. In some villages, sedentary husbands have the opportunity to do sports only when running after an errant or provocative wife. A friend once told me that the best use he had for his wife was her role as the supplier of neighbourhood gossip. She offered him more details than any local radio station would. Another important role wives play is to serve as punching bags to grouchy husbands, although some African men would rather use them as beasts of burden.

So, while waiting for my wife, Gladys to come up with another assessment of the uses of a wife to a husband, I would go ahead and bring out aspects of what I have been doing to save friends from trouble created by females.

Chapter One

Kimbi Gets a Wife at Last

Kimbi was a very close friend to me. He was so close that he always found it normal to drink beers on me without ever bothering to give back. He was blessed with the aptitude of providing good company, packed with fake stories and anecdotes, while other less gifted raconteurs but good listeners footed the beer bills. Whenever Kimbi called on me, I knew my wallet was going to lose weight. He was always so jovial so carefree that he gave you the pleasure of giving him.

One Friday afternoon Kimbi shuffled into my office, not looking as sprite as usual. What further shocked me was that he invited me for a drink.

"Have you inherited from a rich uncle?" I quipped in surprise.

"No." he replied morosely.

"You have started gambling then. Did you win a jack pot?" I demanded rather lost.

You don't win a jack pot that takes you close to the status of Croesus, and rather look as if you have lost your manhood.

"You won't accept my generous beer offer?" he muttered

"Don't go around looking as if you have been hit by a road compactor. Tell me everything right here." I said encouragingly.

"I need a stiff drink," he retorted "and right now. I am a nervous wreck! A good for nothing fellow! A hopeless man without balls."

Kimbi fidgeted with his tie nervously and smiled like one of those guilty guys, who after fighting bravely in court to prove that they are innocent, are still given a hard sentence by an uncompromising magistrate, and started moving out of my office.

I realized that he really needed the stiff drink, and that it would be useless trying to get him to talk sense without one. I wheeled him out of the office and on to my car, and drove off towards Chvu Bar, our popular after work spot, where I recommended a double tot of cognac for him. I then pulled him over to a private corner and tried to calm him down.

"Now," I said looking straight into his eyes. "You must have a real problem haunting you. Have you lost your job, gambled away your family fortune or murdered somebody?"

"I have fallen in love." he murmured simply.

I reeled at this statement and for a split second suspected Kimbi had gone Loco. Love was supposed to be a good thing, although many African men actually never fall in love. A friend once told me that only women are supposed to fall in love. A man simply wants a good woman, pretty enough to be by his side, and with whom he can have sex and make children. That is why polygamy is common. Falling in love on the other hand means being weak and this school of thought believes that women always take advantage of the love sick. However, I am on the side of men who believe in love.

"Fallen in love? But that is a good thing. Men in love are supposed to float in the air, smile like a satisfied baby and perform back summersaults all over the place. On the contrary you look like a bloke who would remain down cast even if the biggest clowns in the world performed in front of him. Cheer up my friend, love is a good thing. You are on your way to a wife and children. That means a family."

One would have thought that Kimbi would brighten up by this brilliant speech. I did not actually expect him to dance jigs and say 'ole', but he was exaggeratedly on the gloomy side.

"Look," I said rather sternly "if you would calm down, take time and tell me all about your new found love, then maybe we could work out something."

He exhaled air like a deflating football, looked at me as if he expected me to perform a miracle and opened up.

"Akoni, do you believe in love?"

I decided to ignore the question. It reminded me of my friend Nsom, who has always held that love brings a lot of wickedness, and he has several facts with which to substantiate his point. According to him, women should love their husbands, but it is very dangerous for a man to love any female. According to him, a polygamist should treat all his wives impartially, equally and fairly, but would become partial if he developed love for one of them. He also insists that love has led many men to behave foolishly, fall out with their family members, ruin a family business or even abandon work in pursuit of a woman, and worst of all misappropriate public funds just to satisfy the caprices of an over demanding but loved dame. I may not agree with him fully, but I have seen a few strong men break down into tears in front of a female, either pleading for her love or for her fidelity.

Kimbi seemed to have discovered that I had dodged from answering his question.

"So you are also among those fools who never want to talk about love and rather consider it with derision?" he asked angrily.

"Is that what you think?"

"Your attitude makes me to think that you are one of those fellows whose wife was imposed on him by parents."

"I am rather waiting to hear your story." I was already full of impatience and was almost regretting why I had abandoned urgent work to come and face the rubbish that Kimbi was putting forth.

He seemed to realize that foolishness has its limit and continued.

"You see, I met Nakoma a week ago." he stopped and looked round as if he expected her to appear.

"Yes?" I prompted "Is she beautiful? Charming? Attractive?"

"All of it sir." he said with surprising force. "Nakoma is perfect, just what it takes. She beautiful, charming, attractive, gorgeous, everything hat the ideal woman should be. "

It was as if I had tuned to a radio station where one of those haranguing pastors is struggling to cover as much time as possible by repeating ten times, every sentence of the little material he had managed to organise for the day.

"And her smile, what else would a man want?" he continued.

I understood that this Nakoma in question had directed cupid's arrow straight into my friend's heart. He had been struck by the thunderbolt as love sick chaps often declare.

He snorted loudly and continued, "Since then I can't stop thinking about her. I can't sleep. I keep imagining her as my wife."

I realised that if not checked the love sick bloke would go on and on, and decided to put an end to this foolishness.

"But you are not married." I pointed out. "All you need to do is to propose to her and make her your wife."

Even an imbecile would have imagined that this was the simple and straight forward thing to do, but Kimbi rather shuddered and looked at me like a donkey that had been hit by a refuse van.

"Come on man," I continued. "Propose to her. That is the reasonable thing to do. It sticks out like a sore thumb."

"Akoni, you have to see her, she is perfect, God's prettiest creation. Do you expect me to just walk up to her

4

and say 'I love you, let's get married'? She would laugh derisively at me and say 'Water seeks its own level.' No! I don't think I will ever have the guts to press my suit to her."

Kimbi was a strong man, one of those guys who always boasted that girls swooned upon beholding them. We had always attributed his continuous bachelorhood to the fact that cash could only flow towards him and rarely away from him. None of us in our circles could ever have suspected that this jovial prattler could melt in front of a female.

"Would you rather have me speak to her on your behalf?" I proposed

"No!" he interjected viciously. "I will not have her considering me as weak. Besides, I don't trust you. How do I know whether you won't go fixing things for yourself?"

"I am already happily married." I reminded him.

"Well I suppose so, but one can never be too careful." he concluded.

If not of the fact that he looked half dead already I would have landed him one on the jaw. Imagine the selfless sacrifice in promising to intercede on his behalf, being interpreted in that distasteful manner. Anyway, man must make amends to drowning friends. After all, some married men have been known to flirt from one woman to another like a bee from blossom to blossom. But such frivolous behaviour cannot be attributed to a man like me who always wants to do the right thing.

"Since you take it that way," I replied, "I suppose you try solving the problem yourself. Have you tried talking to her?"

"I am just coming from her place. I have made a few attempts to confront her already but I wonder whether I would ever be able to say anything to her. When I see her all the courage flows out of me. I feel like a chick facing a hawk without a mother hen to defend it. I am sure I can never go further than grovelling at her feet."

"But you are a man. Women want strong men and would not fall for weak stuff. Put your head up, push out your chest proudly and say the word." I advised.

"What word? I can only confront her with a gaping mouth while all words escape. I will only end up concentrating on some absurd topic."

"You mean the weather?" I asked.

He eyed me morosely and made no reply.

"But the words 'I love you' are the simplest words to say. No body can kill you for that."

"You are just saying that because you managed to convince your wife to marry you. Maybe you trembled in front of her like a child with fever when you were proposing."

I had always placed myself in that class of tough eggs who confront women with confidence. I am sure if I were one of those blokes who attempt to chat up every female they meet, I would have had a long queue of them waiting to give me satisfaction. However, God puts certain limits to things, so smart guys like us are naturally of the reserved nature. Kimbi's words therefore hurt me some.

"There you go insinuating things that would shock even my wife. Well, since you seem to have come to ridicule me instead of getting good advice, I'd better leave"

My attempt to stand up was thwarted by a violent thug on my arm.

"You want to wrench off my arm?" I said plaintively

"Please don't go." whispered Kimbi. "I will settle down and become as meek as a lamb. I am all ears."

I felt a lot of pity for the lovesick bum.

"Let's settle down to brass tacks and look at it this way. You love this woman very much?" I asked

"Absolutely! Completely! With all my heart" the radio pastor again.

"But you cannot sum up the courage to press your suit?" I continued.

"That is putting it mildly. I am totally scared about the whole thing." Kimbi replied.

"Then," I said with emphasis, "Why don't you follow the example of this Russian fellow they called Lenin?"

"He too lacked words with which to chat up a wife? But he was a genius." Kimbi was surprised.

"Yes, he was a genius and a busy man too." I said. "He had very little time for frivolous pursuits such as chatting up women."

"Then how did he end up exchanging gold rings with that wife of his? Nadyeshda Constantinovna Krupskaya was her name, right?" enquired Kimbi.

"Quite right! I am even surprised that you know her name. You see, Lenin was the communist boss in the struggle against Tsarist Russia. Krupskaya was one of the top female fighters who worked closely with Lenin. It is alleged that his heart bit fast each time he wrote instructions for her to execute, and her heart bit even faster each time she received and read through these instructions. Lenin, it was alleged did not know how to open up to Krupskaya, suspecting that she might stop considering him as a strong leader and rather ridicule him as a weak man who could be influenced by the mere charms of a woman. For her part Krupskaya did not imagine that such a hero like Lenin could relapse into the weakness of loving a woman. One day, she was therefore pleased to read at the end of a very businesslike correspondence from Lenin the simple statement, 'But why don't we get married?' Her heart throbbing, she carried out the task assigned and sent back a thorough and well inspired report, at the end of which she added, 'Concerning the marriage proposal, why not?' You see, it was so simple, no dragging of feet, no poems, just plain understanding." It was really quite simple.

"What a smart way to propose without having to waste time, corner a fellow, drag your feet in front of her and develop high blood pressure through fright that she might rebuff your advances." Kimbi said.

"True. It is said that Lenin had a brain bigger and heavier than ours. His brain weighed about two kilograms as opposed to one and half kilograms for an average adult."

I was sure, I had read about this somewhere.

"Is that so?" asked Kimbi "Then he must have had one of those massive heads."

"It was not wonderfully massive," I replied "but there was quite a prominent forehead."

"One would wonder how this Krupskaya fell for a bloke with a head like that." Kimbi said "I guess those Bolshevik females spent their time and effort plotting to overthrow monarchs ordained by God to rule them, and so could not see straight."

"I suppose so." I concurred.

Like those Pastors I have always been admiring, who, when they grab a topic, would not want to let go until they have spent at least an hour on it, Kimbi continued flirting with the Lenin topic, gaining time to look for another line of conversation that would make him forget his love sick state.

"Krupskaya. What a foolish name. What does it mean? Why not go for British names with meaning like Underwater, Underwood, Drinkwater, Woodman or Churchill." He said.

"I would rather prefer simple and less jaw breaking African names like Tsvangarai, Umslopogaas or Ravolomanana" I pointed out.

Kimbi remained thoughtful for a while and seemed to be digesting the feasibility of the Lenin approach. But as we say, most excellent theories have a flaw and Kimbi put his big toe right on it.

"Your story states that Lenin and his wife had a relationship as colleagues and regularly exchanged correspondences. Lenin simply took advantage of the situation. How do I add marriage proposals to correspondences when Nakoma and I are perfect strangers to each other?"

"But you could send her a letter. Just give me her address and I will take the letter to her myself." I said reassuringly.

"And if she refuses? Have you thought of the possibility that she might broadcast my request to all the girls in her office and laugh at me from those delicious lips? No I won't take that risk." Kimbi was firm.

I could have pointed out to Kimbi that Nakoma's mates did not know him and so all their childish giggles would have no effect on him, but he looked so determined to make his case difficult that I offered the simplest option.

"You have to make an attempt some how. You win some, you lose some. My wife, Mawomi was not served to me on a golden platter. I also had to take the chances of getting accepted or rejected." I pointed out.

Kimbi did not look convinced by my eloquence. He looked more like a deaf mute who was taking advantage of his impairment to shirk his duties. I was exasperated by this attitude, and concluded that I should table any suggestion that came to me.

"You could consider the option of sending her flowers or strumming on a guitar below her window every night?" I proposed.

"You think we are in France or Spain?" he replied crossly "Play a guitar indeed."

"Try other ways then." I continued despite the negative countenance "We can arrange and I attack her. Then you rush in as the hero and save her. That one cannot fail, but remember not to hit me too hard."

"If you frighten that queen of maidens in any way I will hit you so hard that you will never forget it." He said threateningly, "Why can't you think of something better?"

I felt I had tried my best and could congratulate myself. Opting to act like a mad man and attack a dame just to get her hooked up to a friend is not done easily.

However, good chaps like me hardly give up when it comes to getting friends out of tight situations. Lesser men would have turned to their beer bottle, or given some flimsy excuse and buzzed off. We rather stick to the last when it comes to helping our fellow man.

"From every indication there are only two things you can do." I said "Either you sweeten your tongue with honey, corner Nakoma somewhere and make her understand that you consider her as the best thing God has put on Earth."

"Or what?"

Kimbi was quite a blockhead.

"Listen!" I advised "Just walk up and present your aching heart to her. She will likely receive it and place it by her own. All females wish to have a cherished heart ticking by their own, and you know what?"

"What?" Kimbi asked gruffly.

"Many of them end up frustrated because it is rather the men who take the chance of offering their hearts to them. A

10

woman is thus lucky when she is proposed to. Offer your heart to her and she will receive it happily." I said smiling encouragingly.

I had never imagined that I could come up with stuff like that. If I had been performing on stage, my audience would have been clapping continuously and asking for an encore. Instead of applauses however, I got but a gloomy look from Kimbi.

"And if she drops it?" he said dully.

"Drops what?"

"The heart of course!" he barked "What was I supposed to be presenting to Nakoma?"

"Why would she want to drop it?" I asked.

"Don't you see that my heart is too ugly and dirty to be beside hers?" The love sick Kimbi wailed.

"Don't be a fool. If she drops the heart, then pick it up and present it to her again. That is what they call insistence." I was working hard.

"And if in anger she dashes it to the ground so hard that it shatters?" Kimbi insisted.

"Pick up the pieces, take the heart for repairs and present it to another woman. For God's sake, there are many beautiful dames idling around who just need to be proposed to." I said curtly.

"Did I tell you that I needed just any female? I am in love with Nakoma and I want only her." Kimbi was really difficult.

"Then propose to Nakoma instead of babbling like a child." I said heatedly.

"I will not be able to, I am too scared." Kimbi said weekly.

"You therefore need Dutch courage." I proposed "Take a few tots of whisky, acquire some boldness, and act. That is why some guys go on drugs, but drugs are not good, so try alcohol."

"I think you are right" he said beaming. He called for a few more tots, was generous enough to offer me another bottle of beer and armed himself with courage-giving alcohol. After gulping down his tots he was now transformed from a whimpering blighter into a chap who could easily take on a lioness. He tapped me on the back generously and shoved off to his conquest. Great conquerors like Alexander the Great and Napoleon would have had something to learn from him.

With that kind of confidence, a man cannot fail to get results. Women are like sitting ducks just waiting for the right words to hit them like cupid's arrow and compel them to fall in love, or say 'yes.' I only hoped that my friend would meet Nakoma in the right mood and sail through.

I was reclining on my favourite couch in my sitting room, armed with a glass of cognac and enjoying the prattling and laughter of my children. My wife, Mawomi was bustling all over the place arranging and rearranging things. My mind was shifting from the children, hunched in front of the TV to the good suggestion I had given to Kimbi. That was an idea worth a billion francs which I had just dished out without presenting a bill. At least they say the best reward is the gratitude shown by the beneficiary of your good action.

Just then there was a loud knock on the door and bless my soul as I observed Kimbi shuffling in, looking as if all hell had broken loose. He did not appear at all like a chap who had come to show gratitude for a sound advice given to him free of charge by a concerned chum. Neither did he have the air of the Duke of Wellington, after he had just returned victorious from Waterloo. But what the hell, I thought. He was supposed to be celebrating a new found love, not looking like a rejected soul. He could easily be likened to an undertaker who has just received news that cure for AIDS and other deadly diseases had been discovered and was being circulated free. I found it difficult to imagine what must have happened. A young man who left me yesterday full of Dutch courage and bent on capturing a life partner, looking like a small weakling in a class of bullies.

"You surprise me Kimbi." I said with meaning.

"I rather think I need all the sympathy in the world" he replied morosely. "Is that cognac you are having?"

Without bothering to ask for permission, he poured a tall tot of my expensive cognac into an empty glass from which I had drunk water.

"Courvoisier, is it?" he asked, after a very generous sip. "The French can never be beaten in this aspect. Even the Armenian cognac which Churchill loved so much can never measure up to this stuff."

I could see clearly that the bozo was just trying to put up some tough talk. Probably the presence of the children was rather disconcerting. I pulled him out to the veranda where we could speak freely.

"Why are you looking as if you are not yourself? What happened?" I questioned.

"Brother," he moaned "would you imagine that I have made a mess of it?"

"A mess of what?" I asked, fogged.

"Everything! I strode boldly to her house, meaning to tell her I fancied everything about her and wanted her as a life partner."

"Then?" I was eager to learn what transpired.

"In my drunken state I banged on her door, a bit too loudly I admit, but that was supposed to mean that I had control of the situation."

"Oh yeah?"

"Don't say 'oh yeah' like that." He whined. "It is just like saying 'you damn fool', or 'you bumbling gook.' "

"Alright, just go ahead and tell me what happened." I said, more calmly.

Kimbi took a generous sip of the cognac, strode back into the living room and refilled his glass. Then, he came back, taking another sip as he got to where I was standing. I wanted to remind him that he was helping himself to expensive cognac, not cheap beer, but was prevented by the fact that he started talking first.

"She swung open the door with her pretty face distorted in anger." He said.

"Even in anger her face was still pretty?" I could not help asking.

"As pretty as ever." He replied emphatically.

"And you mean she was angry just because of a little banging on her door?" I fired another question, in a bid to sympathize with a good friend.

"Don't call it, a little banging." He said protectively. "She had every right to be angry. You don't virtually break down the door of a pretty fellow and expect her to welcome you with all smiles."

Kimbi, I concluded, could be one of those lover boys who could spend their time running errands for a loved one, even if the errand involved doing things for another boy friend of hers. I couldn't argue with him.

"So you said you were sorry?" I enquired.

"Rather." He replied guardedly.

"Rather?" I asked. "I hope you did not go ahead to show her that you were in control."

"I was totally confused." He whispered

"Confused? You were supposed to be pressing your suit." I said, rather annoyed.

Kimbi simply sighed and continued.

"I immediately became very sober. I apologized profusely but could not say anything else."

"How did you explain the reason for your visit then?" It was interesting to know.

"I said I had missed my destination." He replied. "Yes, I remember mumbling something about a wrong address and regretting having knocked on the wrong door. The excuse was very lame but that was all I could think of with that confused state of mind."

"Pure hogwash" I admitted. "Look", I advised, "You will never go through this, your self. Give me the address so that I help you out."

"With your hopeless ideas?" He snorted. "Look what you got me into. Dutch courage my foot! What ridiculous thing do you think you can tell her?"

I concluded that there was no use getting him into my plan. Smart guys like us always move a step ahead while slow chaps like Kimbi tend to drag us back when we involve them. My plan was simple and ingenuous; I would look for Nakoma, whoever she was and put her straight. I would tackle her like the tough guy I am and make her understand in no uncertain manner that she was putting my friend's man hood to the test. I would then proceed to tune her to operate on the same frequency as Kimbi. What a superb plan. Shakespeare would never have thought of this in any of his best masterpieces.

The next day I dressed to kill, put on the FM perfume reserved for such special occasions and made a bee line for Nakoma's office address, which I had obtained from Kimbi with a lot of difficulty and tact. Immediately I got in, I understood why Kimbi was panicking about what would happen if Nakoma rejected his advances and broadcast every detail to her colleagues. The place was swarming with young girls, clearly suggesting an atmosphere of gossip and ridiculing of unfortunate young bucks. One smallish fellow with reddened lips and a screechy voice was recounting to the others how she had stood down a chap who had been following her around like a fateful dog. 'I told the hound he was not even fit to lick my feet, let alone touch my hands.' she was saying 'And you know what?' she had continued 'he looked at me with longing eyes and sighed like a gambler who had missed the jack pot by just one digit.'

I could quite appraise Kimbi's worries about pressing your suit to a girl who worked in such a place, and getting rejected. But blokes like me are made of sterner stuff. We can kick the engine block of a car and dent it.

"Look here," I said to the closest girl who looked like she could easily kick a man in the groin and enjoy it. "May I talk to Nakoma?"

The stern look on her face made me to add hastily. "Please, I don't know her but I am sure she won't mind talking to me."

"What makes you think that" she said eying me curiously.

"Think what?" I asked trying to appear tough.

"That she won't mind talking to a bloke like you? Are you her uncle or a benefactor of some sort?"

"Hey! Talk to me with some respect" I retorted. "You don't even know me."

She seemed to be assessing me, wondering whether to like me or land me one in the nether regions. I stood my grounds like a lion and stared directly back at her. I did not meet my woman and marry her by trembling in front of females. I happen to be one of those tough eggs who do not babble around, giving chances to a silly female to tell you to go straight to the point. We approach these things in a matter

16

of fact way and take off to the next female if the one we are interested in behaves like a deaf mule.

I could see that my tough attitude and hard stare were having results.

The girl pretended to wipe a speck of dust from the computer in front of her, certainly stealing a few seconds to prepare for the attack. Then she probably realized she was dealing with a hard nut to crack, a dominator of the female sex, and not one of those spineless geezers.

"Why do you want to see her?" she demanded.

It was a tough battle but I had won. I always win when it comes to things like this.

"Why do you want to see her?" she repeated.

"That is left for me and her" I replied boldly.

"Go on, I am listening."

I could see that Kimbi had taste. Nakoma took the gravy, although her flashy eyes could frighten lesser men.

"You are Nakoma?"

"Yes sir" she said, rather impatiently "Don't waste my time asking foolish questions. Go straight to the point. I hope you are not one of those punks who trail every beautiful woman they see, even to their work places where visitors are not generally allowed."

"Hey don't rush things" I protested. "You are quite cute, attractive and maybe fun to be with, but I am married."

"Then what are you looking for here in a den of spinsters?" she fired back

"Actually I came here on behalf of my friend" I said.

"Piss off then, I don't have time for intermediaries." She said, waving me off.

"Take it easy dear" I frowned "You have not heard what I have to say and you are already drawing conclusions."

I could see that Kimbi could never have succeeded without assistance in getting the fellow to accept him. A female does not put road blocks across the path of a weak advancing suitor and he still has the courage to press his suit the way those hot Corsican lovers would have done.

"Well, what does this client of yours want?"

"Don't talk as if I am arranging a business deal. I am trying to make you happy by linking you to a nice guy."

The derisive laughter was unexpected. It almost threw me off gear. Had I not been one of those men who can hardly be wiped off from their feet, even by the punch of a heavy weight wrestler, I would have swayed dangerously.

"Who told you that I needed a man?" she attacked.

I would have given up but for the fact that some wise man once said 'When one door is closed, another is opened.' Another popular wise crack states that 'you cannot make omelettes without breaking eggs.' I was now prepared to use any unorthodox methods to get Kimbi and Nakoma holding hands. It was clear that with women like Nakoma, a gruff African approach might be most appropriate. I decided to start with a bit of intimidation and work up to any point.

I looked sternly at Nakoma and said commandingly.

"Every woman needs a man. It is even put in songs by some great female artists."

"Don't be fooled by those musicians" she said.

"And don't pretend" I said. Women long for marriage and children more than men. According to African standards, you are already getting beyond the age where men would be interested in proposing to you. A bit more of this stubbornness and you will remain single all your life. Make hay while the sun shines. This may be your last opportunity of grabbing a good man.

"If I really wanted a man, don't you think I am pretty enough to have attracted quite a good number of men? By now I would no longer be single" she said proudly.

"That is just the point." I replied. "You scare them off with your attitude and negative approach to sincere declarations."

"Should I accept any bloke who approaches me? Attractive women like me should be careful. Many clumsy fellows who assume that they are irresistible make advances repeatedly, I must admit, but so far, no man I really like, has declared anything to me."

"How would they when instead of smiling in a welcoming manner you growl like a tigress which though not yet on heat, is being approached by a horny tiger?"

I observed her closely to see whether my words were sinking in or simply slipping off some slippery surface.

"Like this friend I am talking about," I continued hastily "he simply tapped on your door yesterday to declare his love for you and you almost rendered him deaf with you screaming."

"The only man who knocked on my door yesterday was not coming for me. He had rather missed his way." She said.

"Is that what you think? The fellow had no other intention but to rope you in as a loving companion."

"Then why did the gook not say so and rather started babbling about mistaken addresses?" she asked.

"Is it not clear to you?" I said "He was disconcerted by the rude manner in which you interpreted a simple tap on your door, as loud banging."

"That's a lie!" she protested "The bastard hammered on my door as if he were waking the dead."

"But that gave you no reason to pounce on him like a panther that has discovered that its meal is about to be sneaked away by a stranger." I snorted defiantly.

She was quiet for a minute, probably fuming and wishing she had a large wooden pestle to crack my skull with. I was relieved to notice that she eventually relapsed into a smile and chuckled.

"You mean that the half wit who came to my house yesterday is your friend?"

"My bosom friend, I could even call him brother" I declared.

"He doesn't look bad, only that he needs a few screws tied the right way."

I was encouraged by this statement and pressed ahead.

"Oh no, he is quite balanced. It's just that unlike some of us, he has had very little experience with women, and your attitude on that day threw him off balance. I tell you he is a bright intelligent and interesting young man" I said reassuringly.

"But he looked like he wants his head checked." She said shrilly.

"He is a very good man, a generous man, an understanding man, a…"

"You may stop painting him sky blue. I still think that he is a nincompoop, but he could make a good husband, one that you put under your armpit and make him do everything you want." She smirked.

"Are you suggesting that you want to make a slave of him?" I asked, rather frightened "Listen, I would not want my friend to be a henpecked husband."

"From the way you present him, he already is." She said, smiling broadly. "All I need to do is to shape him into the kind of slave I want."

20

I was further shocked when she added.

"How my colleagues will love to hear this."

I eyed the treacherous jezebel with disdain and I meant it to register. Women are really strange beings. A young buck is ready to propose *his hand and his heart* as the Russians say, to this woman, and here she is, planning to take advantage. There should be a law.

I wheeled round without further speech and stormed out of the choking office. The hysterical giggles of misguided females that filled the office on my departure disgusted me further and I started wondering whether to have pity or scorn for Kimbi.

"You don't want to think of that girl again" I told Kimbi when I ran into him the next day.

"What do you mean by that? I love her dearly" he protested.

"But you can't. She does not love you" I declared.

"How do you know?" he shouted back.

"I mean, she will accept you and transform you into her slave."

"What does it matter?" replied the lover boy "That is what I would enjoy most. What is life worth without me being her slave?"

He suddenly looked at me suspiciously.

"Have you sneaked up to her like the slimy slithering creature you are, and painted me black?"

"Hey", I protested vehemently. "You seem to have very little faith in me."

"And why not? You are capable of anything." He glowered at me speculatively. "Why are you deliberately trying to dissuade me from my life's goal? You want to create a vacuum and fill it with your odious self, I suppose. I would love to see your wife's face when I tell her what a Casanova you are."

I discovered that if I kept insisting on my point Kimbi would deduce completely that I had met his sweetheart, but with the wrong idea. I decided therefore to let him head for his doom. The only ray of comfort lay in the fact that he would not be able to summon enough courage to confront that distasteful female. This thought comforted me for a while but as one would have it, every white cloud has a dark lining. I hope I got this wise crack right, but what I mean is that at the edge of this bliss of Kimeng's cowardice surged the bitter thought that the daughter of eve may take upon herself to charm Kimeng into her devilish trap. Thanks to me, she was now aware of the fact that he was virtually her prisoner, and could easily lure him into her *black widow spider* net.

I went home, still pondering about the treacherous nature of some women, wondering whether my mother could be like that. Wearily, I sank into a chair.

A friend of mine once said that God was not wrong in giving the upper hand in relationships to men. Women in that position could have quickly brought the world to a catastrophic end. Professor Higgins the mentor of Miss Doolittle in one of those masterpieces of Bernard Shaw, was very right when he advised females to grow up taking after their fathers instead of their mothers. He did not stop there and went ahead to recommend that women should always strive to straighten out the mess in their brains rather than always straighten out the hair on their foolish heads.

My thoughts wandered back into the history of the world of treacherous women. Look at Amazons and sirens that trapped unfortunate men into a life of slavery. Look at the way Eve dragged Adam into original sin. Powerful Samson in the bible met his downfall by hobnobbing with Delilah. The queen of Sheba got the wise Solomon to sin against God.

God himself would not trust females as his close aides and placed only male angels around him. He equally sent a son, not a daughter to save the world. A female would have likely bungled the whole thing.

I suddenly came back to myself with a jolt and discovered that my wife was getting me up to go and eat. My consideration for women softened. Here was a beautiful and gentle woman who only went loose when I let myself go with the booze. You see, one must not blame women completely. Weak fumbling men always give women the chance to have a field day. Give a finger they say and a woman would like to take the whole hand.

A week passed during which I stayed away from Kimbi and his foolishness. My main intension was to shove the Kimbi/Nakoma affair out of my mind and enjoy life the way some of the Roman senators did, living from one orgy to another. I drove to my office where I tackled the days work swiftly and skipped across to our popular spot for a well deserved drink. As I strolled in, a voice shouted.

"Hey chump, come over here and join us. You know I have always been generous with you when it comes to drinks."

I turned round at the sound of the familiar voice and saw Kimbi sitting at the far corner. He had a woman with him, and although I could not make her out because she was backing me, I hoped this new acquaintance would make him forget the presumptuous Nakoma.

"A beer would do me good" I said striding towards him.

Just then the woman he was sitting with turned round and smiled. It was Nakoma. She was radiant and quite beautiful. A devil in angel clothing, I thought, determined not to interfere with their affair. I would have sat down quietly and concentrated on my drink but for the fact that she raised her voice in recognition.

"Hey I know this bloke." she said to Kimbi. "He is the blighter that came to my office and told me that you are a nervous wreck."

"He did?" exclaimed Kimbi looking at me menacingly.

"Yes." she said looking very sincere. "He boasted loudly that he is happily married while you are just the type that could be led by the nose by any woman."

I have noticed that while musicians in Europe and America mainly sing about love, most male musicians in Africa often bring out songs insinuating that a good woman does not exist, and they may be right. One of them went on about the intrigues of women to such an extent that he was almost thrown out of his own home by a combination of females, including his mother, his sister, his wife and his daughter.

Kimbi was staring at me as if he would chew me up into bits if he were given the opportunity.

I attempted to calm him down.

"Stay calm chum, you know how women can turn things up side down."

"What I rather know," he snapped "is how blokes like you strut around like pea cocks, ridiculing your fellow men in front of unsuspecting females."

"At a boy." rejoiced Nakoma. "Let him have what he deserves."

Kimbi looked like he would do just that, and then probably remembered that I had always been a good source of beer. He suddenly relaxed and motioned to me to sit down.

"Nakoma has fallen for me," he said tapping her possessively on the back. "So I am in a good mood presently and do not mind stretching my generosity to back stabbers like you."

If I were one of those block headed chaps I would have taken umbrage and caused much unpleasantness to Kimbi. He was lucky that I am rather of a gentle temperament.

"Nakoma is taking off to attend a meeting of University Women. Not so dear?" he turned towards Nakoma and patted her again patronizingly

"Yes dear she answered. "Don't forget to return home early and wash those things I left in the bath tub."

As Nakoma took off, I turned toward Kimbi who was now looking like he owned the world.

"How did you pull this one" I enquired.

"Simple. You know you are not such a fool after all. I decided to have another go at your idea of beefing up the system with the right stuff and confronting her. Going over to her apartment in the evening, I banged on the door."

"Banged? You never learn, do you?"

"Stop interrupting when strong men give you hints on how to get a beautiful woman." he said rather crossly. "I then stood waiting to handle her, summoning up all the courage in the world. She invited me in and simply fell into my arms before I could say hi."

I could see it all now. She had certainly been softened by my earlier encounter with her. On the other hand, she could be operating like one of those sirens coercing him into a prison and finally trapping him to be at her beck and call. What ever it was, Kimbi seemed to be quite happy. He even allowed a few flies to share his glass of beer despite his legendary popularity as a fly swatter.

I concluded that it would not do to shatter this blissful state of mind by spilling out the truth about this Nakoma babe. But still I felt I should tackle the issue some how.

"You have not fallen like a log, I hope?"

"Am I supposed to fall like a feather? I can see you have never loved in your life. When you love a woman you fall for her completely."

"But there are limits." I protested.

"What limits?"

"You can't allow yourself to be turned into a slave. You can't do washing for a woman. Who knows, very soon you will become her cook."

"Who told you I don't want to be her slave? It would give much pleasure doing all her work. You don't want your girl to destroy her manicure or get too tired doing washing and housework."

"But that is not African, a man is meant to be the head of the family and give orders." I said with emphasis.

"That is why you blokes are considered as uncouth. Being African indeed! A good and responsible man should rather carry the family on his back."

"You have a beautiful home, Kimbi, but from every indication, you have moved over to her place." I said sternly. "An African man rather takes the woman in."

"Now, listen." He said to me rather crossly. "As long as it concerns Nakoma, what I do is not your business. I had a house, not a home. Now, I want to build a home with Nakoma. What is wrong with that?"

"All the men and women will laugh at you, especially the women folk. Think of your mother and sisters."

"What have they got to do with it?", Kimbi asked aggressively.

"It is those sloppy romantic novels you have been reading." I said "Why don't you try Chinua Achebe's 'Things fall apart' instead, and see how Okonkwo handles women?"

"I would be damned if I waste my time on stuff like that. I only managed to read it when we were compelled in Sasse College during English literature classes."

When a man wants to reason like a block head, it is not quite easy to turn him round and make him see reason.

A few days later my phone rang and it was Nakoma on the line

"Hi, Kimbi gave me your number. I just want to thank you for bringing us together. He is such a sweet slave, wonderful, obedient and hard working. Ooh, how I do love him."

I thought over it and decided that if the guy was such a jerk, then he should carry his cross and follow Nakoma like a faithful dog. I did not know Kimbi could be such a nut case. Being a slave to a woman when at the same time, other men controlled their females with the small finger on the left hand, is the real description of a henpecked bloke.

A week went by and Kimbi was totally absent from our usual haunts. All the customers of the popular Chvu Bar where most of us spend our happy hours, and where Kimbi was often a popular orator, missed his anecdotes and raucous laughter. Having been aware of his new catch and her exigencies, I concluded that his continuous absence was due to the fact that he was fervently and competently executing his functions as a house help to his fiancée. I thought I should drop by and laugh at him sweating over a pile of dishes, with a pile of dirty linen and muddy floors also waiting for his attention. However good reason prevailed and I went ahead with my own daily chores.

Another week went by and while cooling down with a beer at Chvu Bar, I got another call from Nakoma.

"Hello, did Kimbi inform you about our wedding arrangements?"

"No!" I said, not bothering whether I should attend such a wedding where my friend would become the *lawful wedded wife*.

"Why should he be the one to tell me?" I asked sarcastically. "I thought you were the boss."

"That's not funny." She replied "Kimbi has changed. If not that I have fallen very much in love with him I would have withdrawn from the whole thing. By the way are you the one who egged him into this macho stuff, because I would never forgive you for that."

"Take it easy lady. I have not met your sweet heart for two weeks now." I said honestly. "I rather thought you described him as a sweet loving slave the last time I had the honour of receiving a call from you."

"That is no longer the case. He is still a dear, but started disobeying me two days ago, and you know what?"

"I am all ears" A silver lining seemed to be emerging on the dark cloud.

"He even gives me orders." She said, confirming my suspicion about the silver lining.

"He does?" I said with glee. "I thought he was just an obedient dog, wagging its tail and smiling foolishly while waiting for every command of yours. And you still love him?" I wanted to know.

"Like my own heart and soul." she replied.

I had never thought that people loved their hearts and souls best, but I let it lie. I felt like one of those prisoners condemned to death who has just received a presidential pardon. Everything had worked out fine after all. I did not know what had happened but everything seemed to have worked for the good.

As I dropped the call, I noticed Kimbi striding in. He no longer looked like a lovesick bum, but rather like a cock that has just defeated another and taken over all the hens.

"Hi there." he shouted as if he were one of those military sergeants calling the squad to order.

"You have been missing." I complained.

"That is okay now. I am fully available, emancipated" He looked more like the sparrow after he had slain cock Robin with his bow and arrow.

"I am not sure I understand you." I said.

"That woman put me under a military regime. I did her washing, scrubbed the floor and worst of all, washed dishes."

"Washed dishes?" I was shocked. The things that women do!

"I am sure you wash even her undergarments." I chuckled.

"Wash?" he said fiercely "I have stopped all that rubbish now."

He pulled a chair and sat down.

"She even made me to change my faith and become a member of one of those churches."

"Which one?" I was aghast.

"How would I even remember the name? The churches are so many that if you opened any door on any street in this town, you have a fifty percent chance of strolling into a house of worship."

Kimbi's statement made me realize that I had virtually been moving with my eyes closed. Churches were fast replacing beer joints and business places along the street. Pastors were the best tenants to deal with, given the fact that they paid a lot better and very regularly too.

29

The new situation was that you could live your house to go to church on Sunday and end up entering the wrong one. Anyway, you are always welcome in any of these churches, as long as your pockets are full of cash, and you have that tendency of easily dishing out the cash. A smart government would make much more money levying taxes on these churches, rather than on honest, helpful and useful businesses. The country could easily come out of poverty with the amount of money the government can reap from taxing the activities of these churches.

"Anyway, what happened?" I demanded.

"What happened? The scales fell from my eyes. I was born again."

If he had heard this statement, the pastor of the church that had been imposed on Kimbi would have rather declared that Kimbi had become unborn again.

Kimbi was now bent on making every use of his new found freedom. He grabbed the bottle of beer that had just been placed in front of him and almost emptied it with one gulp.

"I would have worshiped her for ever like a devoted pet," he said, wiping his lips "though I am still under the influence of her charm."

"You still adore her?" I asked.

"Of course, no other female can take her place."

"Then where did this confident break away from the status quo come from?"

"She pushed me to the damn wall. I would have accepted everything gladly but not being transformed into a teetotaller."

"You mean she banned you from imbibing the life giving juice?"

"She was virtually transforming me into a vegetable. Imagine living on this earth for a whole week without a drop of this most precious stimulant. All the love on earth cannot replace it. That is why even Jesus had to change water into wine to keep the ambiance going in a wedding."

I did not know Kimbi could come out with a crack like that, but an embittered soul is an embittered soul. We boozers need our daily doze to keep us going. Deprive us of it and we become unbearable. I remember clearly when Mawomi, rallied her mother and mother in law and they connived to convince me to stay off the stuff. For a whole week I fought hard to comply, but in the end, the strain involved in the attempt was so evident that Mawomi herself finally broke down and congratulated me for the attempt with a bottle of choice whiskey.

My mind came back to the situation at hand.

"So you revolted." I said satisfied.

"Not really. I still did not have the courage to."

"How did it happen then?"

"After a week and a half I could take it no longer, and sneaked clinical spirit from her first aid box into a glass of water."

I thought that was ingenuous. It just shows you what a thirsty man can do.

"Then," he continued "she came in when I was sipping my glass of water and started sniffing like a blood hound."

"I don't see any problem with that."

"She snatched the glass from my grasp."

"You stuck to your glass of doctored water like a tiger I suppose?"

"I was rather confused. I shrieked like a little bambino who sees his milk being spirited away by a bigger bambino."

31

"She handed back the booze to you I would think. She must have been moved by a big man shrieking like that."

"On the contrary, she proceeded to pour the contents of the glass all over me."

"That was the wall, I suppose?"

"The limit! I told her off in no certain manner and threatened to take off"

"You are sure?"

"Quite! That is when I discovered that she loves me. She went down on her knees and begged me to stay."

"That is when you took the upper hand?"

"I discovered that I had been a fool all that while."

I remember a wise saying developed by some Uzbek teetotallers, Moslems no doubt, that if you run out of water, you run out of life. In our circles we rather believe that if you run out of booze, you run out of life. Mawomi was quite aware of that and knew her limits. Nakoma only had herself to blame.

Chapter Two
Kimeng Ends Up with a Faithful Wife

I was recounting Kimbi's love saga to another friend, Kimeng, as we sat over a beer at Chvu Bar, our popular sport.

"It's a good thing Kimbi ended up having the upper hand. Women always want to have their cake and eat it too." he said.

"I went to their house the other day and she was busy in the kitchen making lunch for us while we were doing nothing but sitting on the veranda chatting, and do you know what?"

"Tell me."

"Kimbi still had the guts to call her to come and serve us drinks, whereas he should have done that himself."

"Don't you think he is exaggerating?" Kimeng took a large swig.

"Who knows, maybe she is enjoying it. Some women just want to be married and play the role of housewife. It is even alleged that some women of a certain tribe in Cameroon actually enjoy being beaten up by their husbands once in a while. They believe that any husband who loves the wife very much reacts very jealously and protectively and this is generally shown through beatings. This regular battery also gives the women what to converse about when they sit with their friends and exchange titbits about married life."

"Yes, I think I have heard about that too. The more frequent the beating, the more the woman is convinced that the man loves her. It is even said that the women provoke their men folk into battering them, if the men remain docile for long and avoid any physical confrontation with them." Kimeng added.

"There was this friend who told me that he gives a beating to his wife on monthly basis whether he catches her doing something wrong or not." I said.

"Why would he do that?" Kimeng asked, surprised.

"His idea is that even if she is not cheating, a woman cannot stay for a month without doing something wrong. Since it is not easy to catch them in the act, it is necessary to mete out these regular doses of punishment just in case. This friend also insists that, it is good to establish your authority over your woman constantly and use the beatings to remind her on regular basis that you are the boss."

"Maybe he is right" Kimeng said morosely. "Keeping women on edge and busy compels them to remain faithful. Give them much time and they will grow wings."

I could sense there was something on his mind. He was not looking very comfortable and seemed to be burning with desire to talk. He was certainly trying to benefit from my expertise as a husband consultant, without releasing much about the trespasses of his wife. I could really see that he wanted to exploit my knowledge of the ways of life but did not know how to broach topics of an intimate nature.

He seemed to make up his mind finally.

"Have you ever caught your wife cheating on you?" He asked.

"Mawomi? No! Why? Women are very cunning and you can hardly catch them in the process. You just have to trust them."

"Have you ever suspected her of cheating on you?"

"Most men do suspect once in a while, but it is better to ignore such thoughts and concentrate on positive things."

"I can't. I am sure that my wife is seeing some blighter who works in the National Credit bank. What do I do?"

I realized it was a difficult question.

"You mean your wife, Ansama is enamoured with an NCB worker? What makes you so sure, have you caught them in bed?"

"Her infatuation for him is quite obvious. Even her colleagues are not happy about the relationship. I am sure that her love for him has made her blind about what everybody else thinks."

"If you are quite certain of that, do like one of those Arab Sheiks would have done to a wife who invites a fake eunuch into the Harem. Horsewhip her into a pulp."

"What foolish advice. For God's sake, she is my wife and the mother of my children."

"Then do what Genghis khan would have done. Banish her from your kingdom."

"Still no good. She will simply go over fully to this bloke and I will be saddled with the care of the children."

"In that case, act like one of those Corsicans. Turn on the man and cut off the instrument that is leading him to sin. I think I read some such advice in the bible."

"Hey don't be a fool." Kimeng shouted indignantly. "The fellow is hefty and much stronger than me. He would simply knock me down with a blow."

"Okay then, give your wife an option. Either she drops the louse or you drop her."

"You need to see the guy; he is a top of the line man. He is rich, handsome, drinks Guinness stout and drives a BMW. He is the type of man any woman would fall for. My wife may promise to drop him, but I wonder if she will succeed in doing that."

"Then take it back on her. Look for an attractive girl and also have fun. It is adultery but I think it is justified."

"Have you gone out of your mind?" he shouted looking at me disgustedly. You are advising that I should cheat on my wife? I thought you would present a wonderful solution on a golden platter, rather than go hitting on such absurd ideas."

I would have stood up and left but the soft heart in me prevailed.

I decided to try another chance.

"Are you sure the problem is not from you?" I asked.

"What do you mean?" he asked aggressively.

"Maybe she misses something that she does not get from you and this lover boy offers her in tons." I said guardedly.

"You are not making any sense" Kimeng said.

"Well, you see," I said "some men don't care to study their wives closely, see what pleases or displeases them, understand what they want in bed, and so on."

"I have always made sure that Ansama is satisfied. I make sure she does not lack, I am always early back home, I drink sparingly, not like some of you who could bit Bacchus himself in a drinking bout."

"Is that all you do to keep your wife satisfied?" I asked.

"More!" he replied. "On women's day and on her birth days, I do the cooking and every other work that women do around the house."

I could have laughed out loud but I refrained from doing so. I realized that Kimeng still had to go back to school to learn about what actually satisfies women.

"Let me give you some solid advice." I said. "On such special days, instead of hanging around the home doing useless work, take your wife for a night away from the house."

"Are you sure she would like that?" he asked. "She may think that I am wasting good money."

"She certainly will like it." I said. "Take her to some beautiful hotel, book a nice room and take along tons of aphrodisiacs."

"Aphrodisiacs, eh?"

"Yeah, you need to work hard."

"What a foolish idea." Kimeng said. "What are the sexual boosters for? You are supposed to be with your wife on that special night, not some sex maniac."

"That is where you display your ignorance in these matters." I said. "Women regularly want a certain dose of sex and unfortunately most men are not aware of this, and often leave them kind of sex starved since African wives are often too shy to make the first move. Again, on such special nights, and given the different setting of the hotel room, the woman needs more action. You have to cope with that. A sexually starved woman could be very unreliable."

"I have never quite seen things like that." Kimeng said. "I rather believe that my wife needs me sexually only once a week and that she may take umbrage if I push her for more."

"That is absurd." I said. "Make sure you attempt every night and give up only when she rebuffs you for that night. Then try again in the morning. Also think of siestas at times. These are little things that keep your wife very satisfied and difficult to be swayed by other men."

"Maybe you are right," said Kimeng morosely "but we are talking about a situation that is already there. What do I do?"

"Look, why don't you commit Seppuku?"

"What is Seppuku?" he demanded suspiciously.

"It is one of the ancient ways out of problems, practiced by the Samurai and also known as hara-kiri. The Japanese believed that the greatest disgrace a man could face was to be cuckolded, so what you did to wipe out the shame and show that you were a very brave man was to publicly thrust a sharp sword into your stomach and let all your entrails out."

"But that is suicide" Kimeng said shuddering.

"They didn't look at it that way. They rather became heroes, admired by one and all. It is just like the fanatics who blow up crowds of innocent citizens, believing that they are taking the easiest and shortest route to get to heaven, to be rewarded with a good number of virgins."

"Those Orientals must be sick in the head."

"I rather consider them as real honest believers. They defy those musicians who claim that everyone wants to go up to heaven but not one of them wants to die."

Kimeng did not look like a bloke who would take his own life because of a woman.

"Anyway, I believe God gave us life to live it to the fullest. Dying earlier than your turn is not permitted because your room would not have been prepared despite the presence of many rooms in God's house." He said calmly.

"Then, you intend to spend the rest of this long life that you will surely have, aware of the fact that some Romeo is sharing your wife with you?" I asked.

He shook his head in the negative.

"Have you tried talking to your Pastor to advice her?" My next question was simple.

"Are you crazy? And add another lover to the fold? No! The pastor might rather realize that she is vulnerable and make his own move."

"What makes you think that the move must succeed?"

"Once bitten, twice shy." He retorted.

The situation was quite complicated. A man who was quite convinced that his wife was cheating on him, but apparently not jealous enough to summon the type of anger that enabled others to squeeze their unfaithful lover's neck like Othello did to Desdemona, a man who did not have the courage of sending an unfaithful wife packing like they did in one of those African villages where Alex Haley's Kunta Kinte

38

originated from, a man who did not have the courage to use a tomahawk to break the skull of his wife's lover the way a Red Indian brave would have certainly done, and a man who could not turn to the next woman and declare his love like a true Cameroonian. This was really a difficult case to handle. But tough guys like us won't give up when it comes to assisting the weak, in family happiness.

I had a troubled sleep that night, reflecting on a possible solution to the complex situation. A lesser man would have given up and saved his head from aching. Should I convince Kimeng to simply believe that he was being deceived and that his wife was a good woman and had simply developed a platonic attachment to the banker fellow? Possible, but he might have had concrete proof of her infidelity which he had not revealed to me. Although many women are very good actors, quite a number of them cannot hide their emotions and feelings when in love with another man.

The next day we met again at Chvu Bar, our popular joint, to see whether we could surface with the right thing to do.

"To tell you the truth," I said after a large swig of beer "I am fogged. There does not seem to be any way out of this mess, except you sit up."

"What do you mean by that?" he asked sharply.

"One of your biggest problems is that you lack the balls to put your wife in her place."

I observed him for a short while and continued.

"You must make your wife jealous, she will attack, and then you will counter by spilling all you know about her secret affair. Threaten to add more babes to your collection of girlfriends and she will finally adjust."

"You think it will work?" he looked dubious.

"You are a handsome bloke and many women would be attracted to you. Grab one right away. You may not actually have to take her to bed but let your wife notice you're flirting with her."

"Akoni," he said suddenly "have you ever cheated on Mawomi your wife?"

"Somehow."

"You think it is a nice thing to do?"

"Hell, no! But many men do it for various reasons. Some are just lechers while others look for satisfaction where their wives are reserved and selfish. Some men go even for full scale harlots out of loneliness. Again others do it in revenge when they do not trust their wives. On the other hand many innocent men are lured into the beds of other women by the women themselves, who prove to be very performant in bed, make open advances or entice them with cash."

"And you, what pushed you into it?"

"Must you know all my secrets?"

"It could help me, you know. After all, that is what you are pretending to be doing right now."

I thought that the word 'pretending' was quite inappropriate and was not a fair description of my honest attempts to assist a weak friend. However, it was clear that the blighter was bent on getting my story and the simple thought that it might prop him up convinced me to plunge ahead.

"My friend Chiambeng is very close to me. His wife, Naimbom and my wife, Mawomi are like sisters, real close."

"The beginning of your story indicates that you may be one of those cowards who take advantage of vulnerable friends' wives." Kimeng said accusingly.

"I thought you wanted to here my story." I was rather annoyed at such interruption.

40

"I am sorry, go on"

"Three years ago" I continued, daring him to interrupt again "Chiambeng had a ghastly motor accident where he lost his car and his manhood."

"You are joking."

"Cross my heart."

"Then that must have been a terrible thing to happen to a man. I am sure he took to drinking. That is where many of such bimbos hide."

"Chiambeng did no take to drinking. He rather took to playing tennis and watching films. He could watch films all night long while his wife sighed by his side."

"Poor woman" Kimeng sighed as if he were Naimbom during one of those lonely nights. "You see," he continued "You were right about women wanting their regular dose of sex. I can now see hat women miss sex more than us, although they often pretend. You remember the time I left hospital and the doctor advised me to abstain from exerting activities such as sports and sex for at least a month?"

I nodded in acquiescence.

"When I recounted my plight in one gathering full of women, the aspect of abstinence from sex interested the women most. It was not out of pity for me as you would imagine. They were rather wondering how my wife would cope without sex for that long period of up to a month. So you see, while the men were telling me to cheer up and that a month was not such a long time, the women were insisting that four weeks was quite a long time for their friend to be deprived of sex. At the same time, it did not in anyway occur to the women that I needed any sympathy for being cut of from one of the most delicious things that God ever created."

"So that is what happened?" I asked "And maybe those oversexed women pushed her into infidelity with this banker at that time and it has continued up till now."

I observed Kimeng's reaction and was sorry I had made such a suggestion

"That bitch" he shouted "I would kill her for that. If it were her with an ailment, I would have waited for her to get well. And there she went cheating on me on the least occasion."

I could really see his point and it made my story easier.

"When Chiambeng was in hospital, his wife worked like a beaver to give every care and satisfaction. I read in some book about women being 'ministering angels when pain and sickness wrack the brow.' Yes she worked like a ministering angel. But when Chiambeng finally recovered and no longer needed a ministering angel, Naimbom started thinking of other things. She rubbed Chiambeng's chest every night with the hope that the doctors might have been wrong and her husband would soon become sexually active. After six months of trying however, she was finally forced to accept reality and consider other options. That is when she started coming to my office, dressed to kill and looking very sweet. The visits became even more frequent and I started wondering why she did this. After giving me the privilege of her visits for two months, desperation seemed to have pushed her to extreme boldness. She attacked me for ignoring her the way a fervent Moslem would shy away from pork. She pointed out that I had full knowledge of the fact that she was completely deprived of sex because of her husband's condition. She said she thought I would have understood the reason for her frequent visits and offered to make love to her. She declared that she was of flesh and blood and had the desires that all women had. She broke

42

down into tears and threatened that she would give in to any rascal who came, and I would be the one to be blamed."

"Women will never stop embarrassing us." Kimeng shook his head understandingly.

"Yes! She said, I would blame her for cheating on my friend if I saw her flirting with some bloke, whereas I was in the position of preventing that from happening. I pointed out that what she was proposing could still be considered as cheating but she stuck to her point, the way a reverend gentleman would if at Baptism a baby happened to bawl in protest against some ancient and unattractive Biblical name that a misguided parent is imposing on him."

I hoped that like a fellow man, Kimeng was really appreciating my situation.

"You sent her out of your office I should imagine?"

"I rather attempted to change the topic but she went on about how the main role of a man is to satisfy his wife sexually and if he is not capable, a close friend like me should do it in his place. She then stopped sobbing and calmly convinced me to accept that there was no other option."

"You mean you just sat there listening to that rubbish?" Kimeng asked.

"Please," I said angrily "listen to the end before you judge me."

"Okay, I am listening."

"As I was saying," I continued "Naimbom insisted that I had no option but to become her secret lover. That way, she would remain a respectable but satisfied wife and would take better care of my friend."

"And you fell for that?"

I looked at Kimeng reproachfully. I thought like a fellow man, he would understand my predicament, but here he was making me look like a confirmed Don Juan.

43

"I finally but reluctantly accepted." I said decidedly "It is said that hell hath no fury like a woman scorned, and scorning Nainbom's proposal would have had unpleasant consequences. I therefore decided to consider my relationship with Naimbom not as an affair but as work. I calculated that each time I would mechanically make love, send her satisfied back to her husband, and rush home to Mawomi."

"Bravo" applauded Kimeng "What a story. You still consider this case of adultery work?"

"It has turned out to be different, I must admit. Naimbom is one of those females who could transform a confirmed homosexual into a woman lover. In bed, she does just what you want and knows expertly how to do it. Her smile is gorgeous and while in your arms, she coos like a satisfied female turtle dove when fondled by a handsome male turtle dove."

Despite all the interruptions, Kimeng seemed absorbed by the story. I am sure he was imagining himself too being lovingly handled by Naimbom.

"Continue." he urged.

I obliged.

"On the contrary," I said, noticing that Kimeng was now anxious to hear it all "Mawomi is one of those straight forward types who go about their wifely duties in a matter of fact manner. In bed she makes no special effort to satisfy her man and makes love the way it is recommended in some old fashioned and outdated religious books. One thus misses all the cooing, caressing and complete attention when with Mawomi. Nainbom on the other hand, gives me all of this and more. I now long and wait for each next encounter, with the eagerness a dog which is fed once a day waits for that meal. The good thing about all this is that, our two families have continued to be as close as ever. Mawomi suspects

44

nothing, my friend Chiambeng has been so taken up by his tennis and films that I wonder whether he would have noticed anything even if it were dangled in front of his eyes."

"And you are sure that no body has noticed anything? I mean, you and this Naimbom woman have never forgotten yourselves and let emotion take over?" Kimeng's interest in the story was intense.

After hesitating for a short while, I continued.

"We came close to being caught once, that was when I also had a car accident and broke my right leg."

"Naimbom must have thrown caution to the wind and vibrated all over the place." Said Kimeng, smiling mischievously.

"Something like that. After surgery, as I came to, Mawomi was bustling in the hospital room where I had been installed. She gathered things to wash, told me to follow doctor's orders attentively, ordered me to make sure I ate my food and shoved off without even thinking of giving me a peck on the jaw."

I avoided the look of pity on Kimeng's face.

"Shortly after, Nainmbom, who had been monitoring Mawomi's moves from the safety of the Nurses' Station, rushed in to occupy the liberated territory. She held my hand tenderly, caressed it gently and whispered sweet things into my ear, to the embarrassment of the young doctor and nurse who had just come in to monitor my recovery process. I was struggling to make Naimbom understand that we had company and such an outburst of emotion could betray us, when she declared to the embarrassment of everybody, 'What would have happened to Mawomi and me, if something terrible had happened to you, maybe affected your manhood? And you say I should not exaggerate? God in heaven knows I cannot go through that terrible situation again. Do you realize that I am not as strong as Mawomi?' I turned to the doctor and nurse in bewilderment and murmured something to them about having an explanation to give later."

"Did they ever get the promised explanation?" asked Kimeng.

I avoided the question and continued .

"Despite the dangers involved, Naimbom insisted on bringing me the most delicious meal everyday and feeding me herself. I made sure that I sent food that Mawomi brought, to other less fortunate patients so as to give the impression to her that I was not ignoring her food. When I finally left the hospital, I was lucky things had come back to normal."

"What a story" said Kimeng. "I suppose you have not stopped 'helping' your friend by enjoying his wife."

"What I am doing is what you can call charity work. I am sure that even Mawomi would give me a part on the back if she were aware of the efforts I am making to satisfy her friend."

"I suppose if you caught your wife cheating, it would not disturb you that much because you are already doing it yourself, and with her best friend too."

Kimeng was really a bloke.

"But I told you that what I am doing is not like cheating. Remember that when I had this accident I referred to, Naimbom was first worried about what Mawomi would have done if I were to become impotent, before thinking about her own self. It is God's work."

I shuddered at the thought of Mawomi in another man's arms. Such thoughts hardly go away fast. I pictured her actually enjoying herself better than when making love with me, and responding to every request of the he goat.

"Anyway if I were to become impotent I would allow my wife take a lover. It's just that I would want her to respect me like Naimbom did to her husband. But while I am I still there for her, I would not even want to believe that Mawomi can look another man in the eyes and say yes."

"You are sure that you have never strayed again?"

"To be honest, Mawomi's aloofness in husband satisfaction has pushed me once in a while to think of it. But Nainbom's presence has enabled me to stand like a rock. She has helped me not to falter as it were, so in one way she is a good thing that has happened to me."

"And now you are advising me to take a lover?"

"Don't put it that way. It should not sound as if you were committing a sin. Simply flirt a little with some beautiful women and make your wife jealous. She may adjust."

"And what if she does not?"

"Then just go on like the cock in the Russian story, who while running after a very fast hen on a very cold winter morning, consoled himself by concluding that if he succeeded in catching up with the hen he would warm himself up by mating with her. But if on the other hand he failed to catch up with her, he would have warmed himself up from the exercise anyway" Yes I really thought I had found the right solution.

"If your wife does not change, you would still enjoy the company of the chap you are flirting with. Takes off some stress you know."

"That was a good joke about the cock. How did it end?"

"Don't say 'cock' in that obscene manner. It gives the idea that you have a dirty mind" I advised. I imagined Kimeng cracking the joke in another milieu full of females and stressing on the word 'cock' as he was doing now.

"Anyway," I continued "There was no end to the story. What I can rather tell you is what was in the hen's mind at that particular moment."

"Tell me." he said eagerly.

"After running for a short while the hen discovered that it may have been running too fast for the cock and considered slowing down a bit. But then she thought, 'If I slow down that horny cock will think that I am cheap. On the other hand, if I continue to run too fast the lazy bastard may not catch up with me, and I will miss the fun I would have had under the handsome cock."

Kimeng forgot his sorrows and laughed uncontrollably. Then he said, "Maybe I should listen to you. There is this house maid of my neighbour's that I have been eying for a while. She is cute and would be an easy prey."

"No you will not!" I shouted. "You can't go that low. Housemaids indeed! What you want is a woman of class, one that even your wife would admire. It's only that way that she can feel threatened. A housemaid would rather make you look like a louse in her eyes. Go for a classy woman and you will break her heart. Then break up with the woman and come back to her and she will welcome you like a hero."

"A thing like that will make me a hero in her eyes?"

"Of course women make heroes out of anything, ants, bugs and even cockroaches, so far as it touches them on the right spot.

"You are sure?"

"Quite."

I saw that I needed to convince my friend.

"Let me tell you a story of this woman who started adoring cockroaches because one was made a hero in a story?"

"How can a loathsome insect like a cockroach be adored by any female, even a demented one?"

"You just listen and learn that most females are not normal when it comes to sex and love. Yes. Ma cockroach, just as unpredictable as any female, decided that she wanted a feather for her birthday gift, rejecting all the gold and silver in the world. She refused to consider all the dangers involved in getting such a gift, so pa cockroach was compelled to take the terrible risk. In an attempt to slip into the chicken house and fetch the feather, pa cockroach was almost transformed into a meal by the cock. Pa cockroach however succeeded in escaping with a broken wing, but without the feather. When he limped back to his wife to convince her to make another less dangerous choice of a gift, he was embarrassed to find her determined to have her feather, even with all the dangers involved. Ma cockroach had dubbed her husband a weakling and threatened to break their marriage and transfer to a more courageous cockroach. Their son stepped in to save the situation and promised the unrelenting female cockroach that he was going to get her feather. He added that the big ugly cock should concentrate on mounting his hens and getting people up from sleep, rather than spend time on ridiculous pursuits like guarding chicken feathers. The story continued with the young cockroach making a fool of the cock and taking a beautiful feather home to his mother. This heroic deed by a cockroach earned the insect high esteem in the eyes of this female after she read the story."

"I suppose she started kissing young cockroaches and making a fuss over them."

"Something of that sort."

Three days later, I went over to Kimeng's house with the hope that I would chat with his wife and maybe pick up a few hints that would help solve the problem. As I stepped out of my car and moved up to the front door, I heard shouting in the house. His wife was beside herself.

"You thief! You cheat! You shameless creature!"

49

She was shrieking on top of her voice while Kimeng was crouching defensively by a corner. As I stepped into the house and said hi, she turned and on noticing me, sent a bottle flying towards me. As smart as I am, I ducked and the crude missile, which I am sure, had been brandished for use as a club for punishing guilty husbands, shattered against the wall. There was a lot of energy and fury in this woman and the first thought that came to my mind was to execute an exit move and rush back to the safety of my car. But just then she announced.

"You there Akoni, I will kill this womanizer and end it all."

I would have thought that kind of speech should rather come from Kimeng who had been complaining about Ansama's infidelity.

"Calm down madam," I said picking up some courage.

Ansama looked like one of those daughters of Eve who believe that a guilty man must be punished in no uncertain manner.

"Calm down?" she asked as if the statement did not make any sense. She went further to confirm it.

"This Casanova was openly kissing that old hag who lives a few blocks down the road, and you say I should calm down? Worse still he said that you advised him to do that."

She looked at me angrily and probably discovered that she had not been stern enough with me.

"You silly imp", she added looking more satisfied with the abuse.

I would have told her that the word 'silly imp' was not strong enough to disturb a tough chap like me and that she needed to grope for a stronger word. However, one does not use bellows on a fire that is already wild with flames.

Despite the contrary opinion of a few of my foolish friends, I am sharp and quick to do the right thing. I ignored the furious female and rescued Kimeng from the corner where he had remained hunched like a condemned creature, and proceeded to drag him out to safety. My sharp instincts told me that the fellow needed a breath of fresh air rather than continuous harassment from an uncompromising woman.

"Hey, what are you doing?" she shouted.

I saw that some tact was needed here.

"This guy really needs his head checked. Deceive a good woman like you and transfer the blame on a good friend is not what is expected of man with a sound mind." I replied.

"Are you saying that you and this fool are not up to something?" she asked.

"I realised that fresh air was what my friend needed most." I replied, looking down at Kimeng

'Fresh air' actually, was just a way of putting it, for the harassed husband badly needed an ample dose of vodka or something strong.

I stared at Ansama the way a strong man would stare at a woman he wants to intimidate, but noticed that she stared back unflinchingly. I therefore applied the other option of cajoling.

"I quite understand that you should be angry. We men are aware of the fact that womenfolk often chat boastfully to each other about how their husbands are having affairs with other women, but we equally know that none of them actually wants to catch us in the act."

"What?" she snarled.

I immediately realized that I had said the wrong thing and rushed to make amends.

"I mean, faithful woman like you would not want to see her sweetheart auctioning kisses to every female who smiles at him."

"But he definitely told me that you gave him the advice to go kissing all the women around the neighbourhood."

"The ranting of a weak man, madam" I countered.

I eyed the Kimeng fellow reproachfully from the corner of the eye and continued. "Let me take him out and knock some common sense into him."

I realized again that I had said the wrong thing as I noticed the look of suspicion on her face.

"I don't mean beating him up" I explained. "I simply wish to seat him down and explain to him in no uncertain manner how it is very bad to betray an honest and faithful woman like you."

She seemed satisfied with this and made no move to obstruct our exit.

When I finally placed Kimeng in a comfortable chair at Chvu Bar, I shouted for the barman to make haste and serve four bottles of beer for us to gulp down before taking a decision on how many more bottles of beer we needed to consume.

"Akoni" Kimeng said finally, looking like Job faced with insurmountable problems.

I suspect he would have readily given me all his fortune in gratitude if I gave him a rope to hang himself with. A moment later, he proved me wrong.

"You and your foolish ideas." He looked at me as if he was considering whether to slap me on the face or abandon me. "What a fool I was to ever believe that you could come up with anything sensible."

He took a generous gulp of the beer which I had offered, with no sign of gratitude and rather went on accusingly.

"You have messed my life completely."

I was aghast at the way things were going.

"But she is cheating on you. All you need to do is to tell her not to use that kind of vicious attack to cover her infidelity."

"Where do I get the courage to return home, let alone face her?"

"It is your house and you have every right in it. Go and face her like a man."

"But I can't, I simply cower in front of her."

He looked round as if he expected his wife to surface any moment.

"Akoni I just feel like becoming a politician, one of those smart ones that enthral huge crowds with some of those elaborate speeches. That will compel her to see my importance and capabilities and make her kowtow before me."

Kimeng was actually one of those chaps who would rather receive a generous volley of rotten tomatoes and boos the moment they attempt to make a public speech. The idea of him thus thinking of enamouring females with a super speech was quite interesting.

"You need to think of something else" I advised. But then, Kimeng did not look at all like the kind of fellow who could surface with any bright idea. This made me to consider a different rope which he could hang on.

"Maybe green eyed jealousy is playing a trick on you, whereas a bit of investigation would prove your wife innocent. Go home and apologize to her" I advised.

The next day Kimeng came looking for me.

"All is well and fine" he announced beaming like a school boy who has just succeeded in having his first love.

"You discovered that your wife was innocent after all?"

"No! She is as guilty as Eve"

"Then what happened?"

"I simply used common sense, not one of those wild schemes of yours. I went back to the house and told her I was sorry for what I had done. I pleaded until she forgave me, meanwhile I completely avoided mentioning anything about her affair. In bed at night, I surprised her by asking that we should pray together before sleeping. While praying for God to forgive me for daring to look at another female, I equally asked him to open Ansama's eyes and make her realize how much she was hurting me through her affair with the banker. During prayers, I tactfully mentioned some of the concrete proofs I had, touching her on a sore spot. She felt very guilty and remorsefully subsided into tears."

I imagined the woman who the other day, had looked like a fiend, eager to have her human feast, transformed into a whimpering female. It only shows you that many African artists are right when they say certain things about women. A friend of mine once observed that, if you insinuate the issue of infidelity, or give your woman the impression that you suspect her of an affair, the innocent ones take their time and gently explain to you where they were and what they were doing at the time you thought they were involved in something dirty. On the other hand, the guilty ones do not even wait for you to finish your statement. They flare up in anger and attack you with all the violence that only females can muster.

"You mean that Ansama was guilty after all?."

"She broke down into wonderful tears, went down on her knees and begged for forgiveness."

"And you forgave her just like that?"

"Why not? All I want is to have her for myself."

"You are a brave man. Some of us would…"

"What ever you would have done does not concern me. I am simply a happy man now."

I would have pointed out to Kimeng that I was the one who suggested the bright idea of confronting her, but I should admit that he had put it to her, better than I would have done.

Chapter Three
Kuma's Baby Solves His Rents Problem

It was one of those afternoons when the sun decides that it will not be challenged by any cloud. The scorching sun seemed to smile mischievously at contorted faces that were trickling with sweat. Even those pharaohs who worshipped the sun god, Ra, would have agreed that the sun was exaggerating a bit. Under such conditions, everyone has his way of coping. I opted for a cold bottle of Kadji beer, a decision which even a confirmed teetotaller would have admired and agreed with. As I was sipping the golden juice, I lapsed into thought. My friend Kimeng now had a happy home and his wife had severed the relationship with he banker fellow. Kimbi and Nakoma had just called me from the clinic where I had just been confirmed that Nakoma was pregnant. However, all can never be a bed of roses as my mind came round to Kuma. This bosom friend of mine was in deep shit as he was being threatened with eviction by an uncompromising landlord, just when his wife, Futela was heavy with child. He had phoned a bit earlier, begging me to wrack my wizard brains and come up with a way out.

Although I had helped many friends in solving one serious problem or another, none of them ever acknowledged my smartness afterwards until they needed help again. One of them after benefiting from my timely display of wit, had rather likened my brains to a mess of stale cassava fufu. Maybe, all my attempts to help did not always turn out right, but the intention was always there. One of those religious books, I wonder whether it is the Torah or the Bible, clearly stated that if you admire a lady to the extent that you wished you could see under her skirt, then you would have committed a sin, even though you had not actually touched her. It is only reasonable then to conclude that if you had the good intension of giving money to the poor, and did not do it because you were broke, you still deserved a pat on the back because you had a holy intention. It should read both ways. It is just like I always have the good intention of repaying small loans I collect from my wife, but never succeeding in doing so. She is always aware of my pure intentions to repay, and still extends credit to her needy husband, on the understanding that my intensions to repay mean that I have effectively repaid. As for my friends, they always want to look at the wrong side of things. I should mention here that when these ungrateful fellows surface with their problems, they always use the words 'wizard brain' to refer to my intelligence, and then end up taking credit for any successful outcome.

"At least, you acknowledge the fact that out of your host of friends, I am the wittiest?" I asked.

"I don't know what you are talking about. I have approached you because you are the most capable of diving into those deep pockets of yours and surfacing with a final solution to this problem of mine."

He had dropped the phone at that point, without giving me the chance to tell him about the state of my deep pockets.

To impress his bride, this blighter had gone for an expensive villa, a beautiful thing to behold, and certainly, very comfortable to live in, but rather telling on the kind of lean wallet my friend possessed. When the money he had advanced for six months had expired, forking out the sum for another six months as required by the landlord was not an easy task. He had continued living on credit for another three months and finally, the landlord had contacted the law and given him a deadline. The landlord's deadline was already around the corner, with the sad looming prospect of court sessions and ruthless menacing bailiffs. However, my pockets were as empty as those of a beggar who has not had generous persons passing by his corner for a week. All thoughts as to where I could borrow some money and help my friend had produced no fruits.

The next day, Kuma came over to my house and threw lavish blame on me for not taking his case seriously. If it were your own problem, bags of money would have surfaced from no where. This accusation, though false, made me to wrack my brains to the limit. I was almost giving up when a bright idea popped up from past experience. I now understand why all these lucky fellows who have enough money to make them employers, always harass young job seekers with what I had earlier thought was an unreasonable demand for proof of job experience. To perform well, you always reap ideas from the past. Even the law courts where laws are strictly applied, accept the use of precedence in some cases.

At the mention of a bright idea, Kuma brightened up and was all ears.

I went ahead to satisfy the waiting ears.

"I had this same problem just before my first son was born. I had not been capable of paying rents for two months and my landlord needed his money. I had survived for a short while by staying out of the house when I suspected that the landlord would pass by. Then my boy was born and we came back home from the maternity. The next morning the land lord, who must have placed agents to inform him on my movements, surfaced around 5 am, bent on mayhem. When I was informed of the landlord's presence, I emerged from the room, cradling the new born baby in my arms. All my friends who owe rents and face a landlord full of wrath can consult me. The effect was surprising and complete. The landlord was immediately transformed from a raging bull into a lamb.

Instead of asking for his rents money, he looked as if he would rather reach into his breast pocket and fork out some cash support. Although he did not go that far, probably because he too was broke, he congratulated me like a chum and walked away with his tail between his legs."

You can imagine my annoyance when Kuma, instead of taking in my story and considering my proposal, rather sought to perforate it.

"But we don't have a new born baby." he protested. "How do I surface from the room with a baby when I don't have one?"

"You should have listened completely to my story. My wife was pregnant just like yours is now, when the land lord started imposing his odious presence at my doorstep."

"But the climax came when your wife had already been delivered of the baby. There was a baby available for your strategy to work, whereas my own baby is still inside my wife." Kuma was an obstinate blockhead.

"I know that. What I am simply saying is that you should lay low for a while. Your wife will soon give you a weapon to use for cooling down landlords."

"But before then what do I do? The deadline is around the corner."

"Remember I told you that I applied the disappearing act for a while. Use your head."

"There you go saying stupid things again. You recommend hiding and advise that I use my head. Am I an ostrich which believes that it has fully taken cover when it hides its head? You and your stupid ideas." he said, looking at me as if I were one of those low creatures.

Maybe he had a point. I remember when my son that I had earlier mentioned was twelve years old and another landlord came storming. The presence of my children meant nothing to him and he hurled abuses at me. He even called me, a lazy, untrustworthy, unappreciative, deceitful worm. I wonder where he got all that rhetoric from, but I would admit, he was really digging it in. It was then that this same son who had saved me as a baby had turned and asked?

"But daddy, for all these years, why could you not build your own house instead of renting houses and finding it difficult to pay promptly?"

The landlord had seemed to be pleased with the question and I am sure he would have given my son a pat on the back if my son's next statement had not unseated him.

"Daddy, you get harassed by impatient landlords who even cheat when they are bringing utility bills. We virtually pay all the landlord's bills and repair his house each time."

I was   the one who had given my son a deserved pat on the back.

"Don't worry" I had assured him. "Your mother and I intend to build a real house, not this kind of hut we are living in. We do not want to provide just any kind of house for our bambinos. What we are planning for is something which will make ministers, jealous."

The landlord had snorted and murmured something about people who could not afford to own a mere bicycle but are planning to buy an airplane. Fortunately Mawomi was not around to listen to this kind of scandal, and since I was on the begging side, I let it go.

When I got up the next morning and Mawomi was reading an old book instead of caressing my hairy chest, another bright idea rushed in. This one, I was convinced, was a winner. Plato would not have caught up with this even if he had lived on the best fish for a month. I picked up the phone and called Kuma, who picked up the call immediately as if he were waiting for it. My announcement of having found a solid air tight solution certainly brought back some life into him.

"Bring it out" he yipped "let's hear it."

Kuma was one of those chaps who, when excited had no limits. His wife once told me that the first time she gave herself to him he almost chewed her breasts into shreds, out of excitement.

"Yeah! I said. Choose between keeping the beautiful house and giving up your car." I expected a volley of appreciation from the other end, but sensed something wrong. Instead of a shrill bark of appreciation that one would expect from a patient dog that has just been given the fattest bone, I thought I could rather discern the anguished howling of a dog whose bone had been transformed into stone just when it was about to have its meal.

"Are you out of your mind? He finally managed to say.

"You have a beautiful car that can be sold for quite a sum. I have capable friends who would certainly pay for it and enable you settle with your landlord."

"I have always considered you slightly more reasonable than a louse, but this one is beyond the limit. Sell my car indeed. Do you realize that I will soon be a father? I am sure you expect me to transport my wife and new born baby home from maternity on one of those blasted motorcycle taxis. You are lucky I cannot reach you through the telephone and land you one on the nose."

I turned round to Mawomi for sympathy. I had been out with friends the previous night, over indulging in the products of Bacchus's club. I had come back home so full of beer that it was virtually sloshing behind the teeth. Mawomi had received me with a frown and some sharp remarks. In bed I had attempted to rub her back but she had told me off in no uncertain manner. That was just what I was hoping for anyway because I was really soused and tired. I was grateful for this chance to go to sleep, without it appearing as if I had shirked my marital duty of satisfying my wife in bed.

I was therefore greatly relieved in the morning when she did not pull back her hand violently as I tactfully directed it to my chest, although I was still afraid that she might remember the night's incident and change colours. One good thing with women though is that after giving you a hard time or shouting loudly over a small crime such as imbibing a few bottles of beer, they always remember in the end that you are the main shoulder on which to place their heads and their main source of happiness. After all, through out history women have called their men, 'lord' and given them more than deserved respect. Although Mawomi had little time for things like caresses, she seemed to have a favour to ask from me, so she applied an extra dose on the hairy chest. It looked like all trespasses were forgiven. I had just settled down to enjoy myself thoroughly and like one of those Arabian genii, grant whatever wish she would request, when my phone rang and that bloke, Kuma, was on the line. He had probably remembered some strong words of abuse to apply on me.

"Hello car seller" I answered, in a bid to counter any flow of abuses.

"If that is meant to be a joke, it is a sick one." He replied "I was rather calling to tell Mawomi that my wife, Futela seems to have just gone into labour and will need her assistance. See how foolish your idea of selling cars was. How would I have taken my wife to the hospital, in a pushcart?"

"It was so near already? I thought she still had a month."

"Two weeks" he corrected. "But the baby is coming early."

"Do you see that you can pull the baby gag now and grab some more time?"

"I don't know but we need to sit in the evening and have a binge."

Mawomi wagged a finger at me. Some how women always manage to eavesdrop when their husbands are on the phone. Mawomi had overheard Kuma's proposal to drown me again in Bacchus's holy water that evening.

I turned towards her with a sincere look on my face.

"I will limit myself to two beers only" I pleaded.

These are all ways of making a woman happy. Let her feel that she owns and controls you and all your sins will always be forgiven. Of course Mawomi understood clearly that there was no way I could limit myself to two beers when the stuff flowed around freely, but felt flattered by my plea.

Wives are loving creatures. A wife can spit fire and brimstone on the slightest provocation such as not enjoying the meal she has prepared for you or hitting one bottle too much, but the next moment she can become your reason for living on this earth. Take a strange woman or a simple girl friend out and she would want to empty your pockets before the end of the day. On the other hand your wife is cautious and prefers to be satisfied with just what you can offer. When she cooks in the house, she reserves the best parts for her husband, and always wishes to make him happy. That is why I can always turn to Mawomi when there is need to borrow cash, despite all the accumulated debts.

As we huddled over bottles of beer that evening, and spurred by the idea that we should celebrate Kuma's eminent fatherhood, the boozing was intense, although the merriment was dampened by the fact that Kuma was not participating fully. He looked like one of those chaps who in one way or the other share the labour pains with their wives.

"Look man, you are about to join us. You will be a father soon." I tapped him gently on the laps. "Perk up and enjoy yourself."

The stubborn fellow still looked glum, and I could understand his plight. Many women claim that they are the ones who suffer during child birth. But what is involved here is just a bit of pain which is completely overcome by the happiness of becoming a mother. On the other hand the expectancy period weighs terribly on the man. My friend Kuma was certainly feeling this way which made him down cast. We have all passed through this stage but we have managed it rather differently. Tough eggs like us handle the situation by drowning in the brew and displaying artificial merriment, in a bid to cover every apprehension and anxiety.

"You don't have to be clucking sadly like a hen that has seen all the cocks slaughtered for dinner." I advised "Think positively. Think of the fact that you can now use the new born baby gag on your landlord."

He brightened up a bit.

"Yes," I continued. "You just need to lay low until your wife and child are discharged from the maternity."

Five days later, I went to Kuma's house to tap them on the back for their new baby. I was equally eager to learn how they had managed to convince the landlord to extend the due date for the rents owed. On entering Kuma's house, I perceived the land lord coming out of the toilet. He moved back to the sitting room and with his ample buttocks, occupied the chair that I was heading for. He looked like a landlord who had recovered his rents from the most recalcitrant tenant.

"Thank you for the wonderful reception" he said with a resounding belch. "I think I will take off to my house. My favourite soap opera is coming up. He stood up, smiled benignly at Kuma's wife who was cradling the baby in her arms and shuffled out.

"The baby gag never fails" I said with satisfaction to Kuma "but it seems to have worked extremely wonderfully in your case."

I looked from Kuma to his wife "You seem to have cast a special spell on the landlord."

Kuma quickly understood what I meant and realized that I deserved an explanation. After all we had been working on the project together.

"You and your stupid suggestions." he said, but without animosity.

This type of statement had been directed at me before, and with much bitterness. I had therefore developed thick skin.

"My smart suggestions, you mean. It rather seems to have helped."

"You should not think that you can ever have any good ideas. You led us into big trouble."

I should admit that I was getting annoyed.

"Are you pretending that the baby gag did not work?" I was surprised.

"My landlord's reaction to the baby gag was quite different from yours. He rather looked like he would wrench the baby from my hands and throw it out through the window."

It all came to me now as I realized that people are different. In my case, my landlord's wife had just left the maternity and when he saw my own new born baby, we were like twin souls. It was like a French tramp, sharing his last piece of bread and bottle of cheap wine with a fellow tramp. In Kuma's case I realized his landlord was one of those old chaps who had never fathered a child. He was married no doubt but would not be bothered about babies because he had never had one.

Kuma continued. "I would have been taken out in chains, my wife and my little baby thrown out in the street, and all my property carted out to some bailiff's office."

Kuma finally realized that I was still standing.

"Sit down and have a drink Akoni and let me tell you all about it." He said pointing to the chair that had been vacated by the landlord.

"I am completely at your disposal" I replied.

"This is what actually transpired" Kuma said "I came back home from the maternity with Futela and the new born baby, prepared to confront the landlord. When the dreaded man arrived with bailiffs and police officers, I boldly came out of the bedroom clumsily carrying the baby in my arms. Instead of melting like snow, the landlord rather stood his grounds and ordered the bailiffs to start executing. I pleaded that I had just had a new born baby, but received no sympathy. The landlord completely closed his ears to reason and looked around the house fiercely as if he suspected that the furniture, television and other household items would start disappearing through the window. It was then that Futela came out of the room and approached the landlord with a broad smile.

'Hello' she said.' Is it our saviour disturbing my baby? What has this naughty husband of mine been doing to annoy you this much?'

'What did you call me?' the astonished landlord asked.

'I said saviour, and rightly so.' Futela replied 'Which landlord would have allowed us to stay in his house all this while whereas rents had been overdue? You were aware of the fact that we could not pay our rents all this while because we had a few difficulties, and were preparing for this little angel, so you did not bother us the way other landlords would have. You fully deserve being the child's godfather.'"

Kuma stopped and looked at his wife and child adoringly and continued.

"I watched the landlord melting like butter in front of the unexpected praises from Futela. And you know what?"

"Tell me" I said eagerly.

"The landlord chap did not even object when Futela cleverly added that he was like the patient dog that will eat the fattest bone in two month's time when the outstanding rents will be cleared. Can you imagine that just like that we gained two extra months of grace?"

"The bloke left just like that?" I asked.

"No!" replied Kuma smiling broadly." He dived into his vast *gandoura* pocket and brought out one of those wallets which should have been discarded years ago. Anyway, despite the outward appearance, the wallet seemed to be full of bank notes, money he might have been reserving for the bailiffs. He pulled out a few notes, declared that it was the first time he was being honoured with the title of god father and placed the bank notes on the child."

"Our dear wife" I said to Futela. "What would we do without you? That intervention was very timely and smart."

"A woman can do anything for her baby" she replied sweetly.

"That is not all" Kuma said "Since that day the land lord has come here three times, but not for his dashed rents. He comes visiting his god son as he always puts it."

Chapter Four

Tonain's Daughter Learns the Hard Way

On Sundays, I usually get up from bed a bit late. Then, I put on my jogging suit and tennis shoes and go sweating. Jogging or taking a fast walk is often the only way that fellows, who spend their whole week sitting in an office with mental exertion and very little physical exercise, can keep fit. As I go jogging, I meet other sedentary office chaps who do a catch up on weekends too. At times, I go with Kimbi or Kimeng. While jogging, we pick up remarks from the peasantry who toil from morning to night and from Monday to Saturday, and rest only on Sunday. These sons of the soil often comment openly that we must be crazy jogging under the sun to no particular destination and for no fruitful reason. I remember one of them was bold enough to ask me on one occasion whether I had nothing useful to do, and had invited me to work in his farm instead of engaging in such fruitless pursuits. If an African peasant went walking briskly, he was certainly going to his farm, to a cry die or to some traditional occasion. On the other hand if you saw him running or jogging, he was probably escaping from harassing gendarmes or running after a stubborn and provocative wife, with the aim of administering severe punishment.

On this fateful day, when I got back to the house after my normal Sunday exercise, Tonain, a long time friend from school was waiting for me. He didn't really look anguished but a smart man would have been able to discern that there was something in the air. Tonain was one of those hard men, who work like a beaver when ever there was the chance of making ample profit. He was the type who could carelessly knock down a child on the high way just because he was bent on catching up with a lucrative appointment. Many people are like that. I remember when I was travelling with the priest of some village church on a dusty road as he was rushing to say mass in some out station church and rush back in time to receive some relatives who had expressed their intension to visit him on that day. You can imagine the thick cloud of dust raised as the priest drove fast on the earth road, bent on getting back on time so as not to keep his visiting relatives waiting. Suddenly I had noticed a young woman in front of us, carrying a virtually new born baby and dragging a toddler along by the hand. Normally it would only have been normal for the reverend gentleman to slow down and avoid suffocating the infant, the toddler and the young mother with dust, but he paid no heed to this and charged on. I tried to call his attention to this misdeed, but he only laughed back announcing that it did not bother him. After all, he had said. Many drivers ply that road and the woman should have travelled by car instead of exposing herself and babies to the dust. Just then we had by-passed another vehicle coming from the opposite direction, which was slowing down, probably because the driver had also noticed the woman and her striplings. Tonain would have acted exactly like that priest in order to satisfy his greedy instincts.

"Hello Tonain" I yodelled. "What takes such a chum visiting a desert? There is no booze in the house."

"Man does not leave by booze alone, buddy, this is no time to joke." He said, looking at me like a school teacher who had just received a naughty question from a rather stupid child.

"Well, what's up?" I normally adjust fast.

"It's my daughter Nindum" he said putting on a sad face this time.

"My little Nindum?" I asked.

70

"She has completely gone out of hand."

"How far out?" I asked.

I noticed that the question had not gone well.

"What do you mean by out of hand?" I thought my new question was better.

"Off her rockers! Nuts!" he answered.

"You mean she has stripped naked and gone snapping like a mad dog at fellows in the street?"

"I would punch you in the stomach for that statement" he growled. "Are you insinuating that my darling child has gone mad?"

I would have thought the bloke had put it himself in black and white that his daughter had gone mental. However one does not put a suffering man to the test, so I continued.

"You mean Nindum has gone nuts and off her rockers and but is not stark raving mad?"

Tonain looked at me coldly as if he was considering whether to land that punch on my stomach or not.

"My daughter is not mad. Why can't you sit down and listen instead of rushing to stupid conclusions. Don't you understand simple English?"

I would have pointed out to him that words like "nuts" should not be used when you are talking about a normal loving daughter, but he cut me short.

"Nindum has escaped from the house to a boyfriend"

"What happened, I mean why would Nindum do that?" I asked in bewilderment

"Well, ask her. That is why I came to see you."

I was taken aback. I think I actually reeled. Imagine a hard nut like Tonain, handing over a revolted daughter for me to tame. He must have certainly pushed her to the limit. Serves him right I thought, but refrained from putting it to him.

71

"But she could not have left like that, something must have happened." I said.

Tonain was one of those popinjays who never saw any wrong in themselves. They always think they are right and never sit down to consider things.

"Give me a lead man." I continued "I don't even know where she escaped to and what to tell her."

Even with ample information about her whereabouts there was still the danger of me being manhandled by the man friend she was supposed to have escaped to. Some of these girls escape to their superman and tell them horrible stories about their homes. In a show of gallantry these blokes give them the type of protection a cock would give to a hen, and some of these guys are hefty and quick tempered. An honest man like me, approaching such a superman could be taken for an annoying relative and given a rough time.

Tonain suddenly loosened up.

"I will tell you where to find her. You know that bouncer in Blue moon night club who looks like a cross between Mohamed Ali and Hulk Hogan?"

I nodded, suspecting the worst.

"That is the guy to whom she has escaped. He lives at the end of Wulebemne Street. You can't miss it."

One can never understand what women see in certain people. I mean, why would a delicate young female cling to a mass of muscles, a guy who could crush her like an insect without much effort? The bloke was not even handsome and looked like one of those villains you see in Walt Disney Cartoons. I imagined myself in the grasp of that monster and made up my mind.

"I am not going to go there. You are the father. Go save your daughter, if you think she is in the wrong hands." I was resolute.

"I knew you would chicken out like the frightened monkey you are." he said with disdain.

"But she is your daughter, where do I come in?"

"She calls you uncle."

"Daddy is closer than uncle."

"It is not that I am afraid." he said unconvincingly. Avoiding my eyes he continued. "I can take on that gorilla anytime and knock the breath out of him. It is just that I don't want to hurt my daughter."

"Hurt your daughter?"

"Of course you block head; which woman of delicate nature would stand there and watch her daddy squeezing the life out of the man she loves? You know me buddy. If I were the one to go there I would knock his teeth out and make him swallow them."

"And now you are acting as if you are afraid of Nindum?"

I could see all through the tough guy stuff. Tonain was as frightened as a gazelle sharing the same drinking hole in the open savannah with lions, cheetahs and leopards.

"Are you sure you did not apply your rough methods on her and push her to revolt?" I thought Tonain was hiding something.

"No! I have always been a loving father and could never have been the reason for her leaving the house. If there is any, then it would be from the mother."

Just then the door was flung open and Tonain's wife, waddled in. she was one of those females with an ample backside and a blown out stomach from over eating.

"Has he accepted dear?" she cooed to her husband, apparently not taking any notice of me. Other men would have taken umbrage, but this was a worried woman.

"No replied Tonain. The bloke is too frightened to oblige."

It is then that the distressed Mrs. Tonain decided to notice my presence and turned to me.

"We were counting so much on you. You know that wrestler could beat my husband into a pulp and further add to the stress I already have. Please for my sake just go ahead and help us."

I am a gentlemen and I don't know how to abandon women in distress. Besides, her daughter Nindum was very close and respected me very much. I would be ready to lose an eye and save her if that was the only way. The fact that Mrs. Tonain was not considering the possibility of me also getting beaten into a pulp was normal, and since my own wife was not there to argue on my behalf, I obliged.

"Okay, but you people must give me more information about the situation before I go."

"Why don't you simply go and convince her to come back home?" Mrs. Tonain said, patting me flatteringly on the back. "You want to be my hero."

"I insist on getting more enlightenment."

"Please just go ahead. What happened is rather disgraceful. You don't need to know. A hero operates whether he has facts to go on or not."

I decided to prove to Mrs. Tonain that she was not wrong in calling me a hero.

"Take your sissy husband home and protect him." I said bravely. "I will accomplish the mission despite the lack of cooperation from you."

"He is not a sissy" she retorted angrily. "He is as strong and brave as they come. I won't have you calling him sissy just because you have accepted to do a very small task for us and face that weakling my daughter is with."

By the end of the day, I had done nothing. My mind skipped from strategy to strategy but none was water tight. The shear thought of facing the bouncer fellow made me cringe. To make things worse, Tonain's wife had revealed that their blasted daughter spent the night hanging out with her boyfriend in the night club and during the day it was difficult to know whether the hunk of a man was at home or not. That made it virtually impossible to sneak in and convince Nindum to go back home. My stress was so much that my wife noticed it and asked me what I was mulling over. I simply mumbled something about too much work and pretended to fall fast asleep with a well practiced snore.

I got up the next day still fogged. As I drove off to the office, I resolved that one does not spoil his day with a matter like that. A solution will certainly pop up later in the day. I started wondering whether it was because I had good children or that I knew how to handle them expertly that made it rare for me to be confronted with such wayward juvenile attitudes.

Just then that bright idea that is always hiding somewhere in my brain came out. It was quite easy, why had I not thought of it. The idea was one of those clear and sure ones that would have made that eureka chap jealous. I think he was called Archimedes, if am not mistaken. Yes, Archimedes would have used a far stronger word than 'Eureka' if faced with a similar problem to my present predicament, this idea of mine had occurred to him. Listen to the ingenious idea as you might likely use it one day to rescue an errant daughter or niece. I would go to the house of the bouncer when he was in with Nindum. I would then call her out for a chat. With Nindum out of the house, I planned to hug her closely and start rubbing her back as we conversed, giving the impression to any observer that we were having an affair and I was her sugar daddy. I am a very favourite uncle and knew Nindum would not hesitate to come out when she heard me calling from outside. Of course this would be done with my car packed closely at an escape position, with one eye concentrated on watching out for Hercules. The idea behind all these antics was to raise jealousy in the brute, with the result that he would turn on Nindum and scare her with the beating of her life. I once read somewhere that brutality to a woman has the power of changing her perception of her lover and transforms him from the sweetheart to a hideous character.

Following my plan therefore, I went to my mechanic and made sure that my car was in good shape. I then drove over to the liar where Nindum had taken refuge and bravely rang the door bell.

"Nindum," I announced, "this is your favourite uncle Akoni would you come out for a second?"

As Nindum stepped out, I took her hand and pulled her away from the house, towards my car of course.

"Is he in the house?" I questioned.

"No he went out" answered Nindum calmly. "He will not be back for a while."

The situation was not what I had expected. There was a hitch in my plans. However Spartans like us never give up.

"Come into the car therefore let us talk."

She followed me meekly to the car and took the other front seat.

"What is this I am hearing about?" The question did not seem to bother her

"I have decided to leave my parents, they have become unbearable, and then I met Fultang."

So that was the name of the junior brother of Titan who had captured Nindum's heart.

Just then, the door of the car opened, two hands grabbed me by the neck and lifted me out. Before I could say 'hey', two resounding slaps were administered on my jaws. As I reeled and struggled to maintain my balance, a powerful kick in the groins made me regret the day I was born. Then I saw King Kong picking up Nindum from the other seat as if she were a rag doll and whisking her off to the house. As I stood up, my head was throbbing and swollen, my nose and mouth were bleeding and my tie askew from the rough handling.

I could not go straight back home in that state. I therefore made a beeline for Tonain's and after giving an account of my ordeal, received some first aid treatment and tidied myself up. I could explain the bump on my head to Mawomi, that I had bashed the damned coconut on entering the car.

When I get involved in helping a husband to solve his problems with errant wives or daughters, I always succeed. The problem is that this success never comes that easy and the beneficiaries always end up with the impression that I had no hand in the successful outcome. Actually, many of them believe that it is all their effort. Tonain was one of these block heads. He came to my office the next day, accompanied by his wife and towing Nindum behind him.

"You succeeded in getting her out of the lion's den?" I was perplexed

"Simple as ABC." he replied smiling like David would have done after slaying Goliath. Some of us are not clumsy bumbling fools like you." he continued.

"But how did you do it?" I asked admiringly.

Tonain sat down carelessly and smiled.

"I worked like Sherlock Holmes would have done. I assumed from the rough treatment you received in the hands of the brute that Nindum would certainly receive her share in the house, and I was right. While calling her whore, cheat and all sorts of names he used his belt to chastise her thoroughly. Nindum is not used to that type of brutality of course. We have always handled her like an egg. Besides she was already missing all the luxury and good food." He looked round my office and continued: "I therefore called her and she was sobbing and ready to return home to loving parents. We therefore arranged and when the fellow stepped out, we went over and collected her."

I turned to Nindum.

"So you finally discovered that you were hobnobbing with a brute?" I asked "What actually made you to fall for a monster like that? I am sure after reading 'Beauty and the Beast', you decided to look for your own prince in that hideous creature."

Nindum simply sighed and said "Uncle, I will never try it again."

I was very satisfied with her attitude. It showed that she had completely come out of the infatuation she had for Fultang. From my knowledge of females, she would have flown to his defence and screamed at me for calling him names if she was still enamoured by him. All is well that ends well they say and this was actually the case here.

I thought of pointing out to Tonain that it was actually my plan that had worked the way I had intended and I even got rough handled during implementation, but noticed that the bloke was bent on getting all the credit for the successful outcome.

His wife even went further.

"If my husband had not been such a clever quick thinker, our daughter would still have been in the mess into which you placed her. We asked you to convince her to leave that horrid hunk of a fellow and come back home. Instead, you pushed the chap into administering severe beating on such a delicate child. Do you realize that he could have killed her? I wonder why my husband even brought us here." She snorted like an angry mare.

After glaring at me for a brief moment, she turned smiling at her husband.

"Dear, you were really wonderful. See how we wasted time, pleading with this clumsy fellow to help with the situation, only for you to solve it with your little finger after he had bungled the whole thing. You are the real hero and have always been my hero. I regret having attributed that word to this blighter when we thought he could do something proper for once."

I waited for Tonain to come to my defence but he instead hugged his wife and cooed into her ear.

It was not a new thing for me to work and have others take all the praises, especially when it involved wives and husbands, so I simply smiled.

Chapter Five
Akoni Reinforces His Relationship with Mawomi

It was one of those nights when men dismiss bottles of beer in astonishing quantities and exchange bawdy jokes. One of those nights indeed when barmaids go prancing around from table to table prepared at any moment to receive a slap on the buttocks from a merry lecher. I was already thinking of retiring home to the wife when Bainsi proposed a last drink at a special joint. We thus shifted to this special haunt of Bainsi's and relaxed on a leather couch. As drinks were brought, the scantily dressed waitress moved over to the TV screen in front of us and switched it on. What came up was quite unexpected. Two beautiful fellows were in the process of giving an Arab, a blow job. Then the scene moved on to a group of young men who were using their tongues on some exited females. The women in the scene were enjoying themselves to a climax as the chaps kept lapping expertly. It seemed to give the females so much pleasure that I realized I must have been depriving my wife, Mawomi of something that would make her very happy. I made up my mind immediately. You see, I am of the type that does not move with his eyes or ears closed. I pick up hints from here and there and strive to overcome my wife's reserved nature at every opportunity. I therefore concentrated on the pornographic display and absorbed as much as I could.

Back home that night I proceeded to put into action what I had enjoyed as a voyeur. Mawomi's response to this attempt cannot be described in mere words. It was like offering a delicately baked pie to a girl friend on her birth day, expecting coos of gratitude but rather having the pastry scattered all over your face.. When I attempted to put my tongue to good use, Mawomi administered a solid slap on my face and called me a series of indescribable names. I did not know she had such a solid dictionary of abuses. She finally jumped out of bed and started gathering her belongings, declaring that she would no longer have anything to do with an ardent customer of brothels.

"But I have never been to a brothel" I protested. "What would I want to do with a whore when I have a beautiful woman like you?"

"Then where did you get the obscene idea of trying to apply your tongue on me? That is what those harlots teach you, isn't it?" She sobbed "And imagine that I have been kissing that dirty mouth all this while."

I jumped out of bed and attempted to stop her. The point of a high heeled shoe landed on my head and blood spurted out.

"Don't you try to stop me" she shrieked, deciding not to notice my bleeding head.

Her anger was so forbidding that I decided to let her go and started looking for first aid items.

Where the wife packed off to was unknown to me. But I did not sleep that night. My mind was going over the unfortunate attempt to raise Mawomi to the seventh heaven which had rather backfired. The women in the film were really enjoying it, so why would Mawomi react like that?

I remember I read in some book about how Arab sheiks used to keep huge harems of beautiful women despite the fact that their religion prescribed four wives. In order to make sure that they were the only ones to have access to these sexually starved women, they employed Eunuchs to take care of them. Because they had been castrated and deprived of the capability to have sex, the eunuchs were very vicious, and would inflict serious harm on any stranger caught nosing around the harem. In many cases they equally deprived such young bucks of their manhood. What was interesting in all this however was the fact that these sex starved women whose husbands could not satisfy them because of their numbers, often enticed or bribed these eunuchs into using their tongues to satisfy them. This shows you that the tongue was not only made for licking lollipops or ice cream, or for wagging at unfortunate husbands.

When I met Bainsi Later on the next day, I told him my story which really shocked him.

"But you and Mawomi are quite inseparable. Why would she take umbrage at such a little display of love?"

"That is what I don't know. May be she is in a secret cult that hates tongues."

"That is a stupid thing to say. Does she take away her tongue when she kisses you? I think she is just being prude. She needs a lecture on the uses of the tongue." Bainsi shifted in his seat and continued. "She should have been here to enjoy this story on how the tongue helped this young man who lived at the era of one of those great czars who spent their time conquering and subduing lesser monarchs."

"A tongue helped in what way?" I asked.

"You see, this monarch had a very beautiful and attractive empress, but she had one weakness. She was very obsessed about sex and wanted it as often as possible. She was a nymphomaniac."

"But the czar was always away conquering unfortunate kingdoms. How did she cope? Women always want to have their regular dose of sex."

"That was just the problem. When the czar was away, everybody in the palace, from the nobles down to the palace gardener took turns in satisfying the empress. The czar therefore offered a fortune to anybody who could design a good chastity belt."

"What is a chastity belt?" I had never heard of such a thing.

"It is a contraption that looked like underpants, developed in those days to check infidelity in women. There was a lock in it that was opened with a key. With the belt on, no young buck could have access to he lass. When a daughter came of age, her father would offer her one as her birth day present, and keep the key himself. He only opened it twice a day to enable her ease herself."

"The fathers must have had a lot of work whenever the girls developed a running stomach." I chuckled.

"Such small things did not dissuade strict fathers from ensuring that their daughters remained virgins until the nuptial night."

"How terrible some fathers could be."

"Not only fathers. You had husbands too who imposed it on their wives and opened it only when they wanted her."

"I suppose nobody does that kind of thing these days. Anyway what happened to our czar?" I brought him back to our story.

"He received many chastity belts, one of which rather had a large hole just over what he wanted to protect. He almost had the producer killed for trying to deceive him. The smart man then gave him a strong stick to put into the hole. When the czar did this, two sharp knives came from inside the chastity belt and simply sliced off the end of the stick which had gone in. the man had explained that she could stool and urinate freely through the hole, but anything coming from the wrong side would be sliced off. Keeping the secret to himself, the czar pocketed the key of the chastity belt and buzzed of to one of his campaigns of devastation."

"Very clever of him." I said.

"Yes. When the czar returned from his campaign, he assembled every body he had left behind.. There were counsellors, knights, barons and all the nobility. There were soldiers, servants and everybody who worked around the palace. Each of them was asked to drop down his pants for inspection, and you know what?"

"I am eager to find out."

"Every one of them had lost his penis."

"Everybody?" I was shocked.

"Well not everybody. Just one servant still had his penis dangling."

"He must have been praised."

"Praised? He was given the highest title in the realm and handed over rich estates confiscated from guilty nobles."

"The lucky fellow certainly thanked the czar profusely and sang praises."

"He couldn't. In fact, he was urged by everybody to openly thank the czar for having raised his status from serfdom to the high position of a count."

"And what stopped him?"

"He actually attempted to, but there was no tongue."

"No tongue eh?"

"Yes. He had dived there first with his tongue and when it was cut off, he realized that he would loose his manhood if he attempted further, so he had sneaked off to a peaceful corner."

I wished Mawomi were here to listen to this. A woman is a woman, and of flesh and blood, not a damn statue of marble.

Bainsi did not seem to be ready to give up about the tongue. He smiled at me and continued.

"Of course you should not blame your wife for being angry about your tongue approach. You have never prepared her for that. You see, many women simply consider the tongue as an instrument that men use for chatting them up and which they the women use for ticking off men."

"From now on I will rather reserve my tongue for telling women off." I said angrily.

"You are only saying that because your wife has rejected your tongue. Look! Even tramps know what it means to have a sweet tongue. I once saw a cartoon where a tramp, perched on a park bench, and listening for a while to a young man trying to woo a female by using his tongue artfully to paint things blue, red and green, had advised the guy, and correctly too, that he was quite qualified to go into politics. The tramp had further pointed out that use such a sweet tongue frivolous pursuits like women was quite wasteful.

"We have gone off from the problem. How do I convince Mawomi to come back home?" I asked.

"Make her understand that the tongue has helped many women. Tell her the story of the women in the harem"

"But she would say that the women accommodated the tongue because there was no other source of getting satisfaction. These women were starved. One wonders why a Caliph or a Sultan would want to defy Mohamed and take more wives than he decreed in the holy book."

"Better be careful and stop mentioning Islamic laws of which you know very little" advised Bainsi. "You might misquote something and end up with a squad of suicide bombers on your trail." he warned.

I shivered at the thought of being blown up to pieces alongside some fanatic who was convinced that he had paved his way to heaven.

My mind flitted back to Mawomi, and I wondered what had pushed me into marrying such a naïve woman. Most men make this mistake and end up regretting. Instead of marrying an experienced easy going woman who knows, and is always prepared to do what a man wants, we often go for virgins or women who look reserved and inexperienced. See how a mere attempt at using a tongue as a means of giving Mawomi a special treat had ended. Some of these African wives want their heads checked. Imagine an American president's wife laughing it off lightly when the president was accused of enjoying blow jobs from a secretary. That is the spirit.

I remembered that when we were attending our doctrine classes before marriage, the experienced couple that was preparing us, had talked about love plays and explained that when a couple wanted more fun or had become too old to satisfy each other through normal sexual intercourse, they could use other ways to achieve the same sexual satisfaction. I am very sure our teachers were referring to things like tongues and fingers although they did not come out clearly. What we also know is that the church rejects the use of condoms and what is known as the sin of Onan or coitus interruptus, not the tongue.

Bainsi was in the process of swatting a fly which was bent on sharing his drink when I tapped him on the shoulder and said.

"You are the only fellow who can help me out of this situation."

"What?" he looked at me as if I had suddenly become a Martian

"You simply have to look for this blasted female, where ever she is."

"And order her to go back home, I suppose" Bainsi seemed to be bent on ridiculing me, instead of obliging a bosom friend the way I was always ready to do to them.

"Look, continued Bainsi." We could send my wife, Nabi to handle the issue woman to woman. That would be sure to work."

"No! That will not work. They would just sit together and ridicule me like hell. On the other hand, think man, it is quite simple. Take her out to any place as if your intention is to fix things up."

"And if she refuses?"

"She won't! She wants every chance to tell me off and since she knows I won't come knocking myself, she would want to use you."

"Well, I take her out and what do I tell her?"

"Sit her down in one of those nice pubs and offer her a drink. Then paint me black to her. Tell her all sorts of horrible things about me. That will certainly awaken her womanly feelings and the love she has always had for me. She may break your head with a bottle, but don't worry. She will come running back to me, and you will always be proud that you are the tough guy who rescued the situation. You could even open a consultancy on such issues after that and use me for your adverts."

Bainsi considered the strategy for a while, looking for loop holes.

"And suppose she simply accepts that you are a louse and a cockroach, what do I do?"

"Then add more. Tell her how you have always admired her and have always been dreaming of a blow job from her while you would respond with an experienced tongue display and make her enjoy it the way your wife Nabi usually does. That will make her see that using the tongue in family satisfaction is not so much a bad idea and is frequently done by most families. I would then look like a saint to her."

Bainsi did not seem quite convinced but the look on his face showed that he was considering my suggestion seriously.

When we separated, I went home and slept soundly, certain that Bainsi could not fail. At times I wonder why I had not become a professor. The plan I had given Bainsi was flawless and water tight. All those experienced marriage counsellors would have given applause. Bainsi had agreed to carry out the plan that same day.

Our rendezvous point the next day was at Chvu Bar where I had promised to give him beers and snacks.

Bainsi was late in coming. I had emptied a bottle of Kadji beer and was half way through the second one, when Bainsi came in and dropped his buttocks in the chair opposite me. He did not look like a man who had achieved a feat. Neither did he look like a man who was bearing good news. He rather sighed heavily when I called for his beer and rejected the snack as if I were offering him stale dog meat.

"I hope you did not go and bungle the easy assignment I gave you." I complained.

"Easy assignment indeed!" he retorted "Can anything be easy with a wife like yours? You have just ruined my life. Next time learn to handle your problems yourself."

"What did she do to you, castrate you?"

"Worse than that." Bainsi was beside himself.

"Are you saying that a simple assignment like that was above you?"

"Any more silly questions from you and you will regret why you ever became my friend. Could you listen?"

I deduced that there was much stress in the air and decided to oblige.

He let go two minutes to make sure that I maintained my trap shut and said.

"I called that hopeless wife of yours as we had arranged and everything seemed to be working well. I was terribly inspired. I thought of all the times that you refused to share your biscuits with me when we were in school. I even remembered the time when that girl, Nabuin refused my advances and preferred you. I did my best. I also exaggerated and made up horrible lies. I told her that when we were in school you could not miss stealing anything that was not nailed down. I thought I had touched the soft spot when I said that all the girls thought you were very ugly and demented, and wondered which misguided female would ever accept to marry you."

"She listened to all this and did not break your head with a chair?"

"She rather ordered a drink for me."

"So she instead went bribing you to say more nasty things about me? That devil, I will teach her a lesson."

"If at all you will ever have the chance. Follow my story to the end."

"All right." I gave him all my ears.

"I took advantage of the drink she had offered and now plunged into the real thing. I told her what an error she had made in marrying a dull man like you, who neither knew his right from his left when women were concerned. I implored her to become my lover and I would use my fingers, my tongue and what ever she wanted to give her the happiness she had been deprived of all this while through her marriage to you. She listened quite attentively to all this, offered me another drink and took off."

"Well, that means you got somewhere. Why are you now looking as if all heaven has broken loose?"

Bainsi was supposed to be asking for his promised beers after accomplishing such a job. Although she had said nothing, Bainsi from every indication had worked like a master.

"You have a bad habit of bumping half way into everything. Your wife must have complained to you several times about this."

I could easily understand Bainsi's point. It was just like taking days to plan and develop the best way to tell a woman that her husband had been involved in an accident and died, and instead of having her weeping on your shoulders, she rather breaks into joyous whoops and happily says 'what a break.'

"I thought the story was over. If there is something left, then say on."

"I went home to sleep hoping that things had worked." Bainsi. Continued.

"Worked in what way? That Mawomi had accepted to be your girlfriend?"

"I don't blame you for being edgy. You know I would not touch your wife with a ten foot pole. The point is that I was sure that I had hit the nail on the head, until then."

He looked round like a haunted man.

"My wife stormed into my office thirty minutes ago like a whirl wind and said she was suing for divorce."

"But she cannot be suing for divorce when you have done nothing wrong." I pointed out.

"Every thing was wrong, with me trying to play a good friend."

"Are you saying that I have something to do with it?"

"It is because of your cursed wife, blast her. This morning, your blasted wife made a bee line to Nabi's office and recounted our conversation of the previous day."

"All?"

"All. She described me to Nabi as a serious lecher. She gave her a vivid picture of how I had painted her darling husband black; just to end up proposing to her."

"She said all that?" I asked, aghast.

"She went ahead to say that she had noticed before, how I had always trembled in front of anything in a skirt. Mawomi had continued likening me to one of those Lucifer's lackeys that go around, breaking families. 'You can imagine all the rubbish he was vomiting about my dear husband' Mawomi had substantiated her point."

"Nabi should have blocked her ears to such nonsense."

"She wanted to, but Mawomi was bent on accusing me for calling her darling husband horrible names in a bid to stretch my dirty activities to her. She even advised my wife to be careful or she would end up sharing me with her sisters, our house maid, all the secretaries in the office and any cheap woman who happened to pass around me."

I was really sorry for Bainsi. He looked like one of those liege lords on crusade who left their homes for months and years to defend Christendom against marauding pagans and Arabs, just to return home and find out that their ladies had taken a lover, or worse still developed a close relationship with one of the male servants in the castle.

"You see Akoni, I am now in a terrible mess. On the other hand Mawomi considers you a darling husband, which means that you still have a chance."

I could see his point. Suing for divorce is what females do everyday in Europe and America, but it is hardly done in tropical Africa. Here, our females will prefer to retreat to their parents and give you the opportunity of coming to plead and take them back, after giving up a small fortune to her parents. I remember a friend whose wife abandoned all the luxury and comfort of her marital home and escaped to her parents who were living in a small house with a pit latrine and a fire wood kitchen. After a short while she started missing the opulence and the big mansion she had been living in with all the comfort a woman would wish for. She had abandoned the delicious food items her husband always provided in abundance, the servants who took care of her every demand and her big kitchen equipped with all the modern equipment, to a smoky kitchen and cheap food. Even her father who had received his escaped daughter happily, counting on the small envelope he would get when the husband came knocking, was now worried that the husband was not turning up, leaving the daughter who had now developed expensive tastes, for him to continue feeding and clothing. The rich husband had improved upon the tastes of the daughter and her exigencies would be difficult to cope with. Tired of waiting for the husband to show up so that he could play tough before accepting to release the daughter, the father was now obliged to go pleading with the young man to come and collect his wife. You can imagine the relief on the young wife's face when we eventually went to collect her.

Bainsi called for more booze. We were now twin souls, and I joined him in drowning our sorrows.

Suddenly it occurred to me that instead of ruining my health with alcohol, I should rather exploit the glimmer of hope that had slipped through in the statement made by Mawomi to Nabi, referring to me as her darling husband. I turned and spoke to Bainsi soothingly.

"Things are not quite lost yet. Cheer up."

"You will tell me next to rejoice and clap my hands."

"Not quite that, but think of the fact that Nabi did not break your head with a bottle."

"She should have broken the bloody head with several bottles. Of what use is it to go on living, knowing that I will

93

soon be disgraced in court by one of those damn lawyers who make a living by breaking happy marriages?"

"You won't have to go to court. Leave everything in my hands. As soon as I bring back Mawomi into the fold I will concentrate on your case. By the way, where did you say Mawomi now resides?"

"Go to her uncle's place at Awonjelwi Street."

I drove across town to Awonjelwi Street and parked across the Street from the house of that cursed in-law who would receive and harbour somebody else's wife without bothering to send her back. I hoped to meet Mawomi brooding over the fact that she was not with her dear husband and regretting the day she took such a rash decision to leave.   Emboldened by the fact that she had referred to me as her darling husband, I rapped on the door and waited confidently. The door was flung open by a spoiled brat who looked at me as if I were one of those unwanted visitors that always go around disturbing people's peace.

"Oh! It is you," he said naughtily. "Don't you see you are interrupting my interesting Flintstone cartoon? You are not even welcome here. My cousin never wants to see you again so just go away."

He attempted to slam the door in my face, but I blocked it with my left foot. Mawomi was sitting in a cane chair, reading a magazine. Instead of telling the rude youngster to shove off and allow me to step in, she smiled mischievously, like one of those females in Roman circuses watching the gladiator who had turned down her love being mauled by a lion. I am sure that if she were that disappointed Roman lady and I were the unfortunate gladiator, she would have clapped her hands with much satisfaction as the ravenous beast went ahead to transform me into its meal for that day.

"Mawomi!" I shouted. "Would you seat down and watch this rascal treat me in this manner?"

"He is not a rascal and has every right to send you away." she retorted "What are you looking for here? Go back to your street women."

"But dear, you may hate me for life. Treat me with scorn for all I care. But think of your children. They miss you."

She wavered for a split second. My expert eye noticed it however and I continued.

"Please come home. You love me. Don't forget you told Kimeng's wife that I am your darling husband."

"So that is what made you think that I would just get up and follow you like a meek lamb? I have been a damn fool I all this while, but it is over. You'd better take off before I tell you exactly what you are."

She turned to the willing juvenile.

"Kukwa, make sure the door is closed behind this fool."

As I walked away from the house I felt very bitter with life. This was me suffering because I had tried to introduce something that most people enjoy, to my wife, in a bid to make our sex lives more satisfying, and here was she behaving like a wife who had caught her husband kissing her best friend. As I entered my car and started driving home, I thought I saw Nabi descending from a taxi. She might have been paying a visit to Mawomi with the intension of exchanging tactics on how to rough handle errant husbands. Whatever it was everything seemed to be lost, so I simply drove home.

Having asked my children not to allow anybody to disturb me, I went to my bedroom and had a restless siesta.

I was awakened from sleep by what sounded like merry laughter from the children, spiced with Mawomi's voice. It sounded like a beautiful dream which I tried to enjoy for a

95

while hoping that it will not go away. Then, Mawomi's voice sounded closer as she shook me gently. I opened my eyes in surprise. This was a female who a few hours ago had treated me like something the cat brought in from the gutter, now touching me lovingly as if I had just offered her a gold necklace for her birthday.

"Am I dreaming? Has Satan sent you to torment me further?" I demanded.

"Just keep quiet and listen" she cooed in my ears

Mawomi was not the cooing type, but she did it so well that I was really convinced there was something amiss. May be that lunatic cousin of hers had fallen off a tree and broken his neck, and her uncle needed money in a hurry to take him to the hospital. I prepared myself to act tough.

"What do you want?" I asked roughly.

"Am I no longer your loving wife? Remember I told Nabi that you are my darling husband."

"But you told me to leave you alone."

"That was before the scales fell off my eyes, you sweet thing. Oh how I do love you." She was now passing her delicate fingers through the hair on my chest, a thing she had rarely accepted to do.

"Well, I'll be damned" I said, wishing she would continue with her caresses.

She did. "I am sorry darling, I misjudged you so much. I will do everything to even things out."

"And even accept the tongue?"

"Of course! What a fool I have been."

"Why this sudden change? Did an angel appear to you?"

"An angel in the form of Nabi."

"Explain."

"When you left my uncle's house this afternoon …"

"Leave? I was chucked out by that nasty brat."

"Sorry about that dear, it will never happen again."

"So how did Nabi suddenly become an angel?"

"She had just been talking with her husband. She told me he had escaped from the house when she expressed her intension to divorce him. Then he had bounded back later, transformed from a quivering wreck into a real man. 'Look here!' he had said with a commanding voice. 'This thing about divorce, are you sure you want to go ahead with it?' Nabi had looked at him perplexed, and then without giving her time to reply he had continued, like an army general commanding the troops. 'You can divorce me and leave me in hell but there is one thing I beg of you. Go to Akoni's wife. Let her know that all the things I said to her are false. It was my awkward way of letting her know that Akoni is a sterling character, who loved her so much that all he ever wanted in his whole life was to make her happy. That I am sorry I used the wrong approach and instead made things worse.'"

Mawomi stopped and smiled at me through half closed eyelids, and then she continued.

"As I was trying to digest these revelations, Nabi went ahead to explain to me that the human tongue was not only meant for licking envelopes and honey. God made it for couples to use and satisfy each other. She advised me to stop being prudish and to find out all the things that give my husband pleasure and enjoy what ever he does to give me pleasure."

It all came to me now. While brooding over the situation with Bainsi, I had advised him to confront his wife and make her rather feel guilty.

"You don't need to apologize." I had told him. "What you need is to lap up a reasonable dose of liquor to acquire full command of the situation."

97

It had worked well as it turned out and Bainsi had handled it even better than I had thought. I shoved this into some corner for now and relaxed in the arms of my dear wife.

The next day Bainsi came to my office 'to receive deserved thanks and congratulations' as he put it.

"For what?"

"Your wife and you are sweethearts again thanks to me."

I could not refuse that statement. But my suggestion which he had applied and ended up fixing things between Mawomi and myself had also helped in shoving his divorce situation to a remote corner.

"So you want to drink beer on me because of what you achieved by mistake?" I joked.

Well, all's well that ends well, so I loaded the blighter with praises and invited him for as much booze as he would want to imbibe.

Chapter Six

The Greedy Minister

Mawomi and I were not quite rich but managed what we had well. That is why we were very much admired by my friends like Bainsi, Kimeng, Tonain and Kimbi, who always believed that we were quite comfortable in life. We had sent all our children to the best boarding schools and made our modest home as comfortable as possible. At night, we slept well, knowing that we would get up to a bright new day. One fateful night however, I was snoring as usual, oblivious to all the troubles of the world, when I felt an urgent scratching on my back. As my reaction to Mawomi's scratching was slow, she proceeded to shake me rather violently by the shoulders. This rough treatment forced me to react. I stirred and turned hopefully, assuming that she wanted us to have fun. Instead, she pushed my probing hand away and whispered.

"Listen!"

In the dark, I couldn't see the frightened look on her face, so I continued with what I assumed was the right response to the scratching that she had administered on my back.

"You horny goat," she whispered pushing me away. "I am sure that thieves have broken in."

I was expecting a more eager response to my prompt reaction to what I thought was a suggestive scratching. Instead, she seemed to be alarmed about something. I stopped midway and listened well. She was right. We always made sure our doors and windows were well locked before sleeping, but some how some strangers seemed to have occupied our living room, and from the looks of things were in the process of developing a Strategy on how to smoke us out of our room. We had a modest house, with just three bedrooms. After murmuring for a while, the men of the underworld seemed to have reached a conclusion. A short while later, our door crashed in under the weight of a well packed kick. The doors to the other rooms equally gave way as they were equally battered with heavily shod feet. As I switched on the light, I was frightened by the sight of a brute pointing a gun at me.

"What do you want?" I asked in panic.

"That is a stupid question" Mawomi whispered, taking cover behind me. "You can see that they are thieves. Where is the rents money, give it to them, so that they leave us in peace."

"Get up." the hood loom ordered. "Get up and go to the living room. No tricks or I will blow your heads off."

I turned and looked at my wife and muttered a swift prayer that the beautiful woman should not be tampered with. She looked very beautiful in her night gown."

"But how did you get in?" I asked the thief.

"That should not bother you" he replied harshly.

"But we have nothing that could attract thieves" I said.

"Just do what I say without any hesitation and you will not be harmed."

I got up and dragged Mawomi out to the living room. Just then I heard one of the rough necks complaining from the other room.

"I say boss, there is no one here.

"What? The boss shouted "what of the other room?"

"There is no one here either." The reply came from another cut throat inside the third room.

"What does this mean?" asked the head gangster moving towards me.

Following instructions, my wife and I were laying face down on the carpet in the living room.

"And look at me when I am speaking to you" he said crossly.

"How do you expect me to look at you while I am supposed to lie flat on my stomach with my head down?" I asked.

"Sit up!" he ordered.

"Yes sir" I answered sitting up.

"What is the meaning of this?" the other gangsters had joined him and all seemed to be disappointed about something.

"I don't understand what you are asking about." I replied. If you want to rob us, then take what you want and leave us in peace. If it is cash you want, we have only seventy thousand francs here which is our rents money. Take it and go."

"We did not come here for peanuts like that." growled the gang leader. "You know very well that, that is not what we came here for."

"What did you break into my house for?" I asked confused.

Instead the big brute strode towards me and started choking me angrily. My wife screamed and rushed to help. Another robber jumped in and landed a very powerful blow on her head. As my wife dropped on the floor lifeless, I became frantic.

"Cool down." shouted the villain who had been strangling me. "Chopdie is an expert. He has simply knocked her unconscious. She will be alright when she gets up, apart from a slight head ache."

I shuddered and calmed down a little.

"Now that she is not listening" the chief turn coat said "Where is the daughter we were supposed to enable you to rape?"

101

"Enable me to rape a daughter? But that is preposterous. I don't have a daughter, let alone planning to rape her."

"You don't have a daughter?"

"I have three sons and they are all away in boarding school. The two little girls who were growing up with them have left, one for the convent and the other to school. You could call them my daughters, but they are from different parents. I live here alone with my wife."

"Interesting" said one of the villains. "Then why did you hire us to come and frighten your household and force you to rape your daughter?"

"What?" I was shocked, terribly shocked.

"You forget that you sent Chaibi to come and make a deal with us?"

The gang leader who had been thoughtful for a while said.

"I will give you the whole scenario if you have forgotten. After all Chiabi already gave us three million francs from you for the operation. If you want to back out, you will still have to pay the remaining two million francs for this trouble. After all, a deal is a deal."

"Let me have the story" I said "It may refresh my memory."

"Chiabi came to us and told us that you need special help and that you were prepared to pay five million francs for the operation."

"And what does it entail?" I asked.

"You were once a minister, were you not?"

I ignored that question. My lowly status had permitted me to shake hands with a few ministers, but the possibility of me actually becoming a minister was quite remote. However, since I wanted to get to the full story, I simply waited for him to continue.

"You have been doing everything to be reappointed, but to no avail so far. You have participated in rigging elections in favour of the president's party, you have spear headed the writing of motions of support to the president and paid handsomely to talk over radio programs where you showered praises on the regime, but things have not worked. You have even tried to pass through contacts who claim to be very close to the president but they have rather ended up swindling the little fortune you amassed when you were minister. Finally, you were directed to this witch doctor who gave you certain charms but recommended sex with your daughter as the main thing to do to get reappointed. Having thought over the whole thing, and not knowing how to approach your daughter for sex, you sent your man Chaibi to us. If you don't remember from here, then we will have to force you to remember."

"Look here" I said "I am of lowly status as you can see. A former minister would live in opulence, large house with a large yard full of cars. Look at my living room and cheap TV. Don't you see that I could not be the man you are looking for?"

"You have to convince us more." the bloke said calmly. "Maybe I should finish my story so that you see what I mean. Of course, as a former minister, all your children are already in universities abroad and you live in a big house. If we go there now, your wife would tell us that you have travelled to attend a party meeting in Yaounde. You always give her such excuses when you intend to spend the night here in your concubine's house. Since you pay the rents for this house, it is almost like a second home. Besides you have two beautiful daughters with this woman and one of them is quite beautiful and a student of one of the government high schools in town. You came across to stay in this house for the night so that we

103

break in as thieves and compel you at gun point to have sex with her. Then you would go back jubilant to the medicine man. I suppose you developed cold feet along the line and transferred your daughters elsewhere. We shall collect the rest of our money. You are lucky that we don't have enough time to rape your beautiful concubine."

The situation was quite frightening and the story he had just recounted, was quite unbelievable. How would an honourable gentleman believe in such rubbish from a quack medicine man, up to the point of hiring con men to facilitate the process of sleeping with his own daughter? The things some men would do for power and wealth. Or maybe the fellow had been lusting for his daughter and welcomed this opportunity the way he would have welcomed being reappointed minister.

"Listen," I said seriously. "I have never been up there in society, let alone becoming a minister. I have three boys all in Sasse College. I am a very faithful husband and this woman here is my wife and the only woman with whom I have children. I am quite satisfied with my lowly but comfortable situation in life and I am not bothered about high positions."

"You don't want power and money?" The house breaker asked.

"Such positions of power make you loose your freedom completely. You are obliged to sing praises and pretend even if everything was wrong" I replied.

I observed the thug closely to asses whether my explanations had been accepted.

A sudden thought came to me.

"That is a picture of my wife and I hanging on the wall over there. You can see that I am not lying.

"Pictures don't mean anything" said one of the thugs who had served himself a good measure of cognac that a generous friend had offered me. "You can still take a picture with a concubine and place it in a prominent position in her house to scare away rivals."

"I thought hard again and finally another idea popped out like a jack in the box.

"You could check my documents and see whether I bear the names of the person you are looking for"

"Do you know the name of our client" one of the men of the underworld asked his boss.

"I can't quite remember" he replied.

"Chaibi mentioned it though but I only remember the name starts with the letter N. Lets look at his documents anyway and check hers too.

I was let into my bedroom by one of the thugs, who watched closely as I brought out my national identity card and my wife's. I took the documents back to the bloke in the living room, who examined them closely.

"He is right" the fellow said to the other gang members. None of his names start with the letter 'N' and the woman bears his name to prove that she is his wife. Chiabi must have given us the wrong description of the house."

"What a pity" commented one of the thugs "I was really looking forward to enjoying the spectacle of this bloke punching on his daughter"

"That woman is quite beautiful in her night gown" said an ugly hairy fellow. "It is a pity we knocked her unconscious. We would have had a go at her."

"None of that nonsense!" shouted the gang leader. "We are here for business not for frivolous past times. Let's go."

"We could at least take along a few valuable items." suggested another thug.

"No time to waste" replied the leader "let's go."

I watched them taking off with much relief.

"You don't want to steal anything?" I asked in disbelief. I wanted to be sure.

"We could have your wife, if you insist on giving us something." said the gang leader, but as he was saying this and moving out, I felt reassured.

The hoodlums finally took off and abandoned the door wide open. I quickly rushed to the door to secure it, but then discovered that the lock had been destroyed during the break in. No wonder some people leave behind barricaded doors, with about three huge bolts and large strong locks. I went back to my wife and discovered that she was coming round; she was already stirring and moaning gently. I felt the corner of her head where the blow had landed and it was swollen badly. The brute had not even considered the fact that he was dealing with what is considered as the weaker sex when he was lashing out.

"Sorry sweetheart" I murmured caressing the bump.

Realizing that we were still in an unsafe situation with an unlocked door, I went outside and shouted. After a little bit of hesitation the neighbours poured out of their houses. While the women rushed to help and comfort my wife, the men were running for cutlasses and other crude weapons although it was rather late. At least I was now comfortable that we would have company till the next day when the door would be repaired. These are the advantages of living with people instead of being isolated in your big house, surrounded with high walls and a gate that is rarely open.

I could not make out the blighter who must have hired the thugs. All the men were permanent residents in the neighbourhood and none of them had ever occupied the privileged position of government minister. Since I was sure that the house breakers were not lying, I kept looking around closely for any furtive presence. A teenage girl emerged from one of the houses and rushed to join her mother who was fanning Mawomi with a magazine.

At dawn, the neighbours all dispersed and left us alone. I was faced with taking Mawomi for a medical check and repairing the door. When the carpenter examined the wooden door, he recommended two strong bolts and two locks. I shook my head.

"I want to be safe. Place four bolts and I think three locks would be better."

"If you have the cash, why not?" he replied.

That evening we thought we were quite safe behind our reinforced door, but Mawomi was still a bit jittery. Once bitten, twice shy they say, or do they mean beaten? Well which ever is the word, it referred to my wife's state of mind. For a whole week no thief dared disturb us. On the eight day I even came with a bottle of wine for us to celebrate the situation. After a good booze and having watched our favourite TV programs we retired to sleep. But before that I checked whether all four bolts on the door were in place and whether all the keys in the locks had been turned fully.

As we went into bed, my wife said her usual prayers before going to sleep. I lay by her side, happy that I had a good and comfortable relationship and gave myself up to the usual loud snores of a contented man. I am sure I started dreaming but I cannot remember much. All that came to my mind later was that in the dream, I saw a bloke with a helmet and a moustache. Hitler or Attila the Hun I couldn't quite make out, but the chap strutted towards my house and hurled a bomb at the house. The bomb struck the door and exploded with a loud bang. The bang was so loud that I got up from sleep suddenly. My wife was whimpering by my side.

"They have come again" she said.

"Who?" I asked.

Then our bedroom door burst open and the fellows themselves switched on the light.

"We are back" one of them announced happily. Among the gang of six, I recognized four of the robbers of the other day, but their leader was absent.

"I thought you discovered that I am not the man you are looking for" I asked anguished. "What do you want from me this time? You realize that you almost killed my wife last time."

We are not interested in women today" the new leader said roughly. "All she needs to do is keep out of our way while you comply with our demands without hesitation."

"What demands?" I asked "You know that I am not a rich man. I barely have enough for me and my wife. Last time I even had my rents money which I could have given. Today, I have nothing."

Instead of understanding my position, the bloke growled.

"Now, get up from the bed before I blast your skull open" he was wielding a gun.

As I jumped out of bed wondering what the fellow wanted he continued.

"When we were here on the other mission, we noticed things that could be of use to us. That is why we have come."

"The beautiful woman is quite conscious now too. Maybe we could..."

The ugly bloke who was saying this received a slap from the new leader.

"We had all agreed that we shall not engage in things that will destroy us. Now start packing the things out into the van."

I then realized they had brought a van to clear out everything from the house. But what did I have that would attract them? I did not park my car in front of the house for fear of thieves.

I was now standing by one angle of the room holding Mawomi protectively behind me. The new capo went to the bed and lifted off the blanket.

"Take this and the mattress" he ordered "We noticed that your beds in all the rooms have good mattresses and tiger blankets that could be worth a fortune." He informed me, as his colleagues started packing up the things.

I had sacrificed and bought these items after going for a bank loan. No problem. It was better to stay safe than to cry over things like that. They did not spare our wardrobes either. After my bedroom and the two other rooms, they went to the kitchen.

"Your refrigerator is wonderful" the thief commented. You even have two pressure pots and a very modern gas cooker, and even a microwave. And then your television and deck. You have class. Your carpet and chairs are of quality. How did you get these quality things?"

These things had been given by my wife's brother who had arranged that we could be paying in small instalments. One does not know the worth of things in his house until other people point it out to him. My brother in law had brought these things from abroad where he had served for long in juicy diplomatic positions. He had said he wanted his sister to live comfortably, but had not given the things to us free. As for the past four months, half my salary had been going to him in payment for the stuff. I would admit he had class and the things were good. But in my lowly home only a smart thief would have realized the value of the stuff.

The thieves transported every item from the kitchen and as they were now operating in the living room, I asked the fellow with the gun.

"Have you staged a coup and knocked off your leader of the other day?"

"You have guts" he said looking at me fiercely. "Instead of whimpering like the louse you are in front of fierce men, you have the temerity to ask questions."

"Well, I am curious" I replied.

"Our boss was not interested in this mission, so we had to do it behind his back."

"Even with all the money you got from the ex minister?" I asked

"The old rascal has become elusive since the failure of that day. He has not paid the balance and our boss did not share the dough equally."

Not contented with the loot already packed in the waiting van, the new gang leader checked in the cupboard for the rest of the cognac he had started drinking the other day.

"Drunks" he shouted in disappointment as he noticed that the bottle had been emptied and discarded. "Must you drink everyday?" he complained. I forgot a bottle of good cognac here last time and you could not keep your dirty hands off it? I could slit open your stomach now and remove every drop."

"Sorry sir," I replied "I will make sure I keep another bottle for your next visit."

The turn coat sneered at me and said.

"You and your woman are moving out with us."

"But why?" I asked "You have taken virtually everything we have. Just leave us with our empty house."

"No way" replied the bloke, with a nasty smile "We have taken your phones but you may have hidden one somewhere. Don't worry, it will be a short ride." At gun point, we were led outside to their van and forced to climb in among the loot behind. Four of the hood looms sat with us behind pointing

110

their guns carelessly. However as we moved out of the neighbourhood, the vehicle suddenly stopped and we were ordered to jump down and run. We did just that and the burst of speed that my Mawomi exhibited surprised me.

Back in our empty house, we huddled together wondering what to do. There was no door to lock as it had been broken into splinters. Our mattresses and beds had been carted off, together with our chairs and carpet

"Why would thieves come down to this level?" I complained to Mawomi. "In Europe they are simply contented with money, jewellery and valuable items like pieces of art."

"Our thieves are in the junior league." replied Mawomi, who loved football like any Cameroonian. "We are even lucky that they had not removed our cloths and taken along with the other things."

Mawomi snuggled closer. The heartless thieves had also raided our wardrobe and bundled off any item of clothing that was there.

In the morning we were virtually freezing. Luckily for us our towel and other toiletries had been overlooked in the bathroom.

It took us one month to borrow a few items and put into the house. We now had some cheap chairs in the living room and a cheap television. We had managed to buy a used mattress and bed, through which I developed back ache. However life was going on and our only worry now was that the children would soon come out for holidays and be compelled to sleep on the floor.

We had now gone for a door with metal sheets and reinforced the bolts. We were sure that we could now sleep without fear and our few belongings will stay. But as they say, man proposes and God disposes. I don't want to actually believe that God sent thieves to my humble home. But then, he did nothing to send them elsewhere.

The thieves came prepared. They must have monitored and discovered that I had reinforced the door and replaced the wood with metal. This time they came with a gas bottle and a blow torch. With the blue flame, they quietly sliced through the door and stepped into the living room before we became aware that we had intruders.

We had also reinforced the door to our room. It was now of heavy wood, with very strong bolts to keep it locked. I would have loved to see the shock on the faces of the rascals as they met with such an unexpected obstacle. The chaps pounded on the floor as if they owned the place and ordered me to open up. I recognized the main voice there immediately. It was the ugly he goat that had been bringing up ideas about raping Mawomi.

"What do you rascals want this time." I asked boldly

"Open this door immediately before I get very angry." ordered the house breaker.

From every indication, this ogre was now the leader.

"What has happened to my friend of the other day?" I asked "Have you eliminated him too?"

"Will you close your dirty mouth and open this door?" he shouted

"I will not do that until you tell me why you have come back. Your first trip here was to enable a former minister to rape his own daughter. Then, you eluded your leader and came back for things that you had noticed during your first raid which you considered of great value. You took away those things and left me in misery. Now what do you want again, or did you remember something you overlooked last time?"

I was trying to gain as much time as possible meanwhile Mawomi was making calls of distress.

"You are right there" the house breaker replied roughly. "Those two blokes prevented me from sampling that lovely wife of yours. I have now mobilized my own gang and come back. We are not interested in anything but your wife."

I was fully prepared for them. Apart from reinforcing the two doors I had acquired one of those locally made fire arms, from a craftsman who made unique items.

Just then, I heard furtive footsteps outside. The gravel betrayed the fact that some of the hoodlums were moving towards the window. I was smart enough to understand that while the chief was drawing my attention to the door, the others would be working on the window protectors. I dragged Mawomi off from the bed to the bare floor, but protected by the bed.

"I am already ready for your madam" the gang leader was shouting from the door. "Let me in and I will give her the good time that you will never be able to give."

"You need your head checked" I replied from the safety of the room. "Only female orangutans are fit for an ugly bastard like you to copulate with. You are not even handsome enough for a female gorilla."

The bloke kicked the door viciously.

I had decided to keep my new gun loaded under the bed for any such emergencies. My expert ears told me the other gang members were now working on the window protectors. I lifted the gun took aim at the window and fired. There was a loud howl of anguish accompanied by running feet. Apparently the thieves had not expected me to have a gun. Besides, the locally made weapon sounded like an elephant gun. From the blood we saw the following morning that had clotted all over the pebbles by the window, it was clear that I had hit one of them badly. Anyway, when their chief discovered that I had a gun of an unknown make and all his partners in crime were scampering off like scalded cats, he also took off. I heard the tread of heavy footsteps as they raced off to where ever they had packed their vehicle.

After this last encounter, I was determined that the thieves will not molest my family again. I ordered for two metallic doors and carried out total reinforcement. My wife proposed that we should move from the house and go to a safer place but I pointed out to her that moving would not solve the problem. Besides, we were now so broke that we could not afford that luxury. It was rather necessary to block out all those blokes who could not make a difference between *meum* and *tuum*. Imagine that these blokes had simply decided that all my furniture and household things were theirs and the clumsy ogre had even assumed that my wife could equally be his. I bought another gun, this time a pistol. This way I could fire the two in succession and give the impression that I had a gun with several rounds. I even taught Mawomi how to load the things. Our locally made guns were like muskets that were used by the American resistance against British troops somewhere down the corridors of history. After a volley of fire, you had to reload.

I boasted in neighbourhood drinking spots how I had acquired two elephant guns of six rounds each and claimed that it could scatter a man to bits. This little exaggeration was destined for members of the gang or their agents who may be lingering in the neighbourhood scouting to gather information before they strike. I thought with all these reinforcements and safety guarantees I would sleep like a lamb at night, but this was not to be. I seemed to have developed insomnia from fear and each time I managed to snooze off, Mawomi would shake me up, on the pretext that she had heard some noise outside. However, for three weeks we were not disturbed.

Then one night she shook me up violently. I had actually managed to drift into a sound sleep and would have actually barked at such disturbance if I had not immediately discovered there was something amiss. There was noise outside, a woman shouting but certainly not in our home. This time the thieves seemed to have opted to try their luck elsewhere. The knowledge that I had a gun may have dissuaded them from risking it to my house when there were other easier targets in the neighbourhood. I immediately jumped up and went for my two guns.

"It is quite risky dear." whispered Mawomi "Please don't go out."

"I simply have to go." I declared "I am a good neighbour and all neighbours should be friends in need."

"But dear," Mawomi protested "It may just be a way to lure you out into the open."

"I have my guns." I declared opening the door, a process that took some time because of the combination of locks and bolts.

As I stepped out of the house carefully, I heard a car taking off in the distance. Wailing and shouting was coming from a neighbour's house, the only house with its lights turned on at that late hour. I quickly realized that it was the house of the lady who had two girls in their teens, all students. They lived in that house with two other relatives. It was generally held within the neighbourhood that some big gun was paying for her house and providing for her daily bread. She was virtually like a wife to him because of his regular visits to her house. Mawomi and I, knew very little about the neighbourhood and generally kept to ourselves. We thus had only scanty details about our neighbours.

Having noticed that the thieves or who ever was causing distress had driven off and the woman was now free to call for help. I became bold. Mawomi had put on warm clothes and followed me outside, the brave woman.

"It seems that one of the neighbours has been robbed" she whispered. "The noise is coming from the house with lights on. It belongs to a certain woman" we did not even know her name.

"Let's go and see" I said bravely. We moved over to the house and entered. We did not need to knock on the door or wait to be invited in. The door had been smashed open. I was quick to observe that property did not seem to have been stolen. The TV was on its stand and the chairs and carpet were all there. Then, I noticed Mawomi rush to a teenage girl lying on the floor. She was clearly in pain, and blood stains around her groin gave the impression that she had been raped by the hoodlums. A man of about sixty five years old, in pyjama was sitting on a chair with his head in his hands. A visitor, I thought wondering whether he was a relative or a sweetheart. As my roving eyes diverted to a wall, a prominent picture of the man was dangling there. The whole neighbourhood knew that this woman was not married. I thought I noticed blood stains around the fly of his pyjama trousers, but it could have been anything.

Mawomi had transferred from the child to the mother of the girl, who it appeared also needed ministering. I stood there with my two useless guns in my hands. We heard noises outside an indication that other neighbours were coming. The woman and the man surprised us by their action. She stopped wailing and they both hastily carried the girl who had certainly been defiled, into a bedroom. The other neighbours filed in and were surprised to see only Mawomi and myself. Just then however, the woman of the house emerged from the room.

The man too came out and slumped into a chair. He was looking more guilty than frightened. I am sure he realized that he had made a mistake by coming out and exposing himself to everybody, as he suddenly jumped up and rushed back into the safety of the room.

"Where are the thieves?" asked a plump neighbour. He was wielding a cutlass, but from the looks of the bloke I could guess that he was one of those blokes who would have rather capered off and left his whole family behind if thieves had come but to his house.

"Where are the thieves?" he asked again and seemed now to realize that he was asking a stupid question since he was getting no reply.

The woman of the house had ceased shouting. They had herded all the other members of the house into their rooms and did not really want to attract attention, from every indication. I am sure the lady was now regretting why she had reacted with so much noise that could attract the whole neighbourhood.

"Nothing seems to have been stolen." commented a woman in a strange and comic night dress. During occasions like this one gets embarrassed at the type of things some people wear to bed.

"We are sorry we got you up." the woman of the house was saying. When the thieves knocked down the door, I could not help shouting with fright. That seemed to have scared them off."

"They just took off like that?" enquired a bearded neighbour. "It is unbelievable. You must have frightened them some."

"We are sorry." replied the woman. "You people should just go home and sleep. We are grateful for the fact that you showed concern and came to our assistance."

117

"But where are the children?" a female neighbour asked "Several girls live in this house. "You want to say they slept through the noise?"

"They are not here" the woman lied. "I sent them to their grandmother."

"But what of your broken door? How are you going to sleep?" demanded a bachelor neighbour.

"You neighbours cannot stay here because of us. We shall sleep in our room and lock the door there. I am sure the thieves will not come back." The woman said.

"Well, if you say so" I said, realizing that there was something fishy and the woman certainly wanted all of us out of the place. I made every effort to lead the neighbours away.

"That woman seemed to be very eager to go back to bed with that old goat. I am sure she wants to get enough of him before he goes back to his wife" I overhead a stout neighbour commenting to his wife, as they branched off to their home.

I couldn't quite get her reply for I was equally hurrying to my own warm house.

Once we got in, I secured the door and led Mawomi to bed. Whether you accept it or not the best way to discuss with your wife is to lie in bed close to each other and chat.

"What do you think? I asked when we were ensconced in bed.

"I am sure those thieves raped that little child" she replied. "The child was really in pain and the blood was still fresh. The lower part of her night gown was soiled."

"Why would they not say so if the girl was raped?" I asked

"Some people are not that open." she replied "besides who would want the whole world to know that her daughter had been raped?'

"So that is why they transferred her in a hurry to the room when they heard the others coming?" I asked.

"Sure." Mawomi replied "We are the only ones in the neighbourhood who actually saw what happened."

I remembered the blood stains I had noticed on the fly of the old bloke's pyjama trouser and wondered whether I should tell Mawomi what was on my mind. But why not? I decided marriage is sharing.

"Have you ever seen that old bloke in that house?" I asked.

"A few times. He stops there often, I understand, but I never knew that he actually sleeps there. I wonder where he has parked his car."

Mawomi rubbed my chest and it felt good.

"Did you notice his picture hanging on the wall at a prominent position, as if he owned the place?" I asked.

She shook her head in acquiescence.

"It is quite clear that we were not the privileged guests that those thugs had decided to honour with their visit right from the beginning. They had actually entered the wrong house. It would appear they had been hired by that old chap in the blood stained pyjamas, who is certainly the ex minister in question, to break in and enable him rape his own daughter."

"What?" Mawomi asked in surprise.

"Do you think that the old fellow we saw in that house could be an ex minister?" I asked.

"He looks like one from the way he dresses and the car he rides in" Mawomi replied "But why would an ex minister want to rape his own daughter?"

"Rape must be the wrong word. Some of these old boys actually lust for their beautiful daughters and would pay dearly to be given the chance to accomplish this type of act.

Some call it, tasting the food you cooked to see if it is nice, before handing her over to a suitor."

I passed my fingers lovingly through Mawomi's hair and sniffed. She smelled good.

"Hey!" I said "You have never mentioned that I look like a very responsible and respectable man, and could easily pass for a minister. You remember that those bandits actually believed that I was the ex minister and were not easily dissuaded from this."

Mawomi laughed and then piped down as she realized she was laughing too loudly in the middle of the night.

"When did you ever look like a minister?"

"Listen to the story before you giggle like a little girl." I said. "From what I could gather, this ex minister has been in the cold for a while and wants to stage a come back at all costs. After spending lavishly on a witch doctor, the crook had declared that he could succeed in getting him reappointed, on condition that he had sex with his own daughter."

I felt Mawomi shiver. Every right thinking woman would.

"That is terrible" she said simply.

"What I don't understand is how this woman and her daughters are involved. Those girls there cannot be his. He would have raped one of the girls in his own home not a concubine's child." I said.

"It's quite simple" Mawomi said "This bloke has grown up children who are all living abroad. On the other hand he has been with this woman for ages and has two daughters with her. I am sure this is our ex minister and the real culprit."

When I got up the next day, I thought I could easily wipe the night's scene from my mind, but it was not easy. I had virtually not slept the whole night. Just as I dressed and went for the breakfast that Mawomi had hastily prepared, I heard a knock on the door. I strode over to the door and worked on our multiple locks and bolts. This was my daily job before I could go out of the house or let anybody in. When it was time to retire in the night I also had to work on the door. It was a man's job, just like women cook, make the bed, clean the house, do the washing and worry about the children. As I finally opened the door, I was surprised to find the honourable gentleman of the previous night standing there. He was nattily dressed this time, not in some old bloodstained pyjamas, but he still looked as worried and confused as the previous night after the rape incident.

"Come in" I said invitingly "I was just having breakfast. Would you like to join me?"

"I am not hungry" he replied gruffly.

He looked round furtively as if all the blood hounds on earth were on his trail.

"Can I see you alone for a minute?" he whispered.

"That is okay" I replied "Come in."

He stepped in, still looking very much on edge.

"Take it easy." I said "I live here alone with my wife. All the children are in school."

The bloke looked round and still hesitated to sit.

"Don't worry." I said "You may feel quite free. My wife is having her bath. You know how women take their time. She won't hear us."

The bloke heaved a sigh of relief and sat down, but I noticed that the weight was still on his chest.

"What can I do for you?" I asked. Then I remembered that I had some brandy in the cupboard.

"Would you like some hot stuff to lift up your spirits?" I asked

"Yeah, thanks." he replied. "A few tots would be of much help, although it is rather early."

I fetched a glass and poured freely, then handed the glass over to him.

He took a few gulps and thanked me.

"It's okay." I said "Now let's hear your story before we get company."

"Let me start by thanking you for cleverly dragging those blokes away yesterday night. I was watching from the darkness of the corridor. You know how lousy neighbours can be. It was quite a relief to see them go."

"I see your point." I replied simply.

"I hope you understand why we had to transfer the poor girl to the room and pretend as if nothing had happened. You don't want to have the whole neighbourhood singing around how your daughter had been raped by hood looms." the bloke said.

The fellow had come across to cover up lapses in the cover up of the incidence of the previous evening and was doing it well. Unfortunately for him I had been upset by the whole thing and did not feel like understanding.

"I am sorry I don't quite know you," I said "and I don't know your relationship with the woman and her daughter."

"I am sorry." he said meekly "I should have explained all that to you already. My name is Nikang. That lady is virtually my second wife and the two girls there are my daughters."

"You are some kind of man of the world, aren't you?" I smiled.

"You are a man." he said "and should understand these things. When ever I have stress with my wife I take solace here. As children started coming, I decided to make it a home from home. You have not noticed me around because I generally slip in when it is dark and I only sleep here when I convince my wife that I am going out on mission."

"So this girl is your daughter?" I asked sternly "Tell me really, who raped her?"

I saw confusion on face. He was mute.

"I asked you a question." I said.

"What question?" he finally said. 'What made you to ask that question?"

"I noticed the blood stain on the fly of your pyjama trouser. Now tell me frankly who raped that little girl?"

The sternness of the questions got him stammering. He looked round the living room as if he was looking for a hole through which to escape.

"You raped her, didn't you?" I asked.

He put up his right hand. "I was compelled to do it by the thugs. They forced me at gun point to have sex with my own daughter." He broke into light sobs.

"That will not help now." I said, still with a stern tone. "You may rather end up bringing out my wife from the bedroom."

"True." he said removing a handkerchief from his pocket and wiping away his tears.

"Now," I said "why did you arrange to rape your own child?"

The question fell like a sledge harmer on his conscience but he struggled on.

"What an absurd thing to say." he whispered back "Why would I want to rape my own daughter?"

"You tell my why you did it instead of asking questions. I know that you arranged for those bandits to assist you in the whole sordid act."

He looked at me with pleading eyes.

123

"Don't forget that those thugs missed your concubine's house and landed here the first time. They told me everything."

"Those bastards!" he shouted throwing caution completely to the wind. "I will kill them."

"Shhh" I warned.

However as usual Mawoni was so involved in her make up process that even the chimes of the Big Ben from close up would not have attracted her attention.

"Now tell me why you arranged to rape your daughter." I said again

He looked very miserable.

"I wonder whether you would understand." he finally said.

"Just tell me." I said encouragingly.

"I was a minister some five years ago, and I had been there for only two years. Without warning a cabinet reshuffle threw me out. I assumed that it would be for a short while as all of us ex ministers of the regime often get reappointed. I continued militating strongly in the party and doing everything even at terrible cost just to get noticed by the president, but cabinet reshuffles have come and gone and I have remained in the cold. I would have been satisfied with the little fall offs that we get during election period and other party events, but my wife seems to be very unhappy about me not being a minister. She has lost quite some respect within social circles such as church meeting groups, cultural groups and within political circles. I love her very much and would do anything to satisfy her."

"Even to the extent of having concubines?" I asked.

"There, don't exaggerate" he said. "I have just that one."

"Okay," I said "let's hear more."

The guy looked genuinely ashamed.

"I was directed to this great medicine man that I was told could work wonders." He finally said.

"A medicine man eh?" I said cynically.

"Hey!" the ex minister said "This one is really great, not one of those cheap amateurs you find all over the place. Well, this guy gave me some strong charms and recommended that I sleep with my own daughter for this charm to work perfectly."

"And you believed in this charlatan?" I asked "You really need your head checked."

The honourable rapist stood up to leave just as Mawomi came from the room. Each morning, she prepared breakfast before going in for her own bath. Now, she was dressed, ready to eat and go to work. The bloke excused himself and took off.

The next day, I closed early and rushed home to Mawomi who generally worked shorter hours. I always thoroughly enjoyed every moment I spent with Mawomi and thus exploited every little opportunity to go home early to her. As we relaxed in the living room, she brought up the story of the ex minister.

"I am still worried about the fact that we are abetting a criminal" Mawomi said ruffling my hair.

"You don't want to jump into something that does not concern you" I replied calmly.

"But raping a young lady, and this is even totally unpardonable because it involves the bloke's own daughter" Mawomi was hot.

"I agree with you completely." I said "Don't worry. God will certainly find a way of punishing him. You will see."

"I hope so" Mawomi replied "I would hate to see such a dirty man go unpunished.

Just then it came over the news flash.

"Honourable Nikang, former minister of the regime died today of a heart attack. This sad event took place at the shrine of one Funyah, traditional doctor and Sooth Sayer…"

What ever information followed, I did not bother to listen. I turned off the radio.

"That is a fellow who would not seek for sound advice." I told Mawomi. "With a serious consultant like me available at no cost, he still had to go ahead and do the wrong thing."

I was later on informed that Nikang was one of the very strong elders in church and every member of the congregation had the impression that he lived a very pious life. Rather, the church should identify such bad eggs and send them far away. These are the type of bad examples that push many good persons away from the church or make them condemn the church at every turn.

I have recounted only part of Nikang's tragic story and that is all I knew up to the point of the death announcement. But I am sure like me, all of you are interested in getting the whole story about Nikang's tragic end. Such stories hardly ever stay hidden and it was no long that I got the full story, a complete narration of the medicine man's latest activities that led to the demise of Nikang. Now, pour yourself a glass of something nice. Kola coffee, Kadji beer or cognac, then relax and listen to Nikang's tragic story.

'The great and popular medicine man that the ex minister was talking about was called Funyah. He was a squat fellow with a greying beard and a bald pate on the head.

Funyah came out of the house and stood expectantly on the veranda. He was dressed in a long white gown with a skull cap. Suddenly the guests he was expecting came in through the archway. These were new customers, two women he had never seen before. From every indication, they were sisters and looked very much alike.

126

"We hope you were not going out." said one of the women.

"Of course not." replied the clever Funyah. "The gods always tell me when visitors are coming. I was waiting to receive you and I always receive honourable guests like you outside before I take them inside."

"You knew we were coming?" asked one of the females.

"I knew two days before that two women were coming to see me today, and as you can see I could even foresee at exactly what time you would arrive."

"This is really a great man." one of the women whispered to the other.

"And quite genuine from every indication." replied the other, also in a whisper.

Actually, Funyah was a fake. He claimed to be a witch doctor, exorcist, oracle and fortune teller. He succeeded by chance once in a while to 'cure' a mad man or forecast correctly, and since his statements were always cloudy any thing cold b interpreted as correct. However, when ever he failed, which was more often, he always had a way out. Either he blamed it on the patient, or some relative or acquaintance, or he developed a very plausible reason that his customers always accepted. The oracles of ancient Greece who were always consulted to predict the outcome of wars would have learnt a lot from him. To further convince his ignorant clients about his capacity to see and know everything before hand, he had located his house a hundred meters from his parking lot. Between the parking lot and his house was a simple footpath arranged such that not even a motorcycle could move on it. All visitors therefore passed through the parking lot and went on foot up to the house. There were trees planted closely on both sides of the path, and in a nearby shady grove, a watch out man was always present. The watchman was armed with a telephone with which he could simply transmit the message giving the full descriptions of an arriving guest. When communication technology failed, this watch out man would rush unseen to the house and inform Funyah of approaching guests. That way, Funyah always came out to wait for the guests, pretending that it was the gods that had informed him of the visit.

The shrine was a simple room that stank horribly of some crude Indian perfumes. There were a few stools for visitors, while Funyah himself sat on a frightening rug made of rabbit skin but disguised to look like the skin of some prehistoric animal. By a corner, strange frightening objects were displayed, some with feathers and hair, some with pricks from the porcupine, and some with skins of snakes and lizards. There were a few skulls displayed too although it was not easy to say whether they were from children or monkeys. Funyah made sure that the shrine looked as frightful as possible. At one corner was a bed that was well made. This was not his bedroom but was placed there to take advantage of naïve female clients.

"Welcome to my shrine." Funyah said to his guests. "There are stools there, you can sit down."

He also sat down on the frightening looking rug and crossed his legs. As earlier stated, although the rug was of rabbit skin, it was disguised to look like the skin of some monster out of one of those frightful African folk tales.

"You have come on an important mission. I can see it clearly." he said rather closing his eyes. "And yes I can help you. It will not be easy though."

The crook opened his eyes and examined the women closely. He could not tell yet which of them actually had a problem, but they were both beautiful women between forty

128

and fifty years of age. They looked well to do and gullible if separated. All his tact was needed here.

"Consultancy is five thousand francs," he said "and as you place the money in the calabash, my gods start seeing the problems you have, through your hands, and start determining which solutions to give me."

He was not saying this to any of the women in particular but he was watching closely. One of them opened her expensive handbag took out the money and placed in the calabash. The clever Funyah now knew who had actually come to consult without asking. He took a rattle by his side, shook it near the ear of the woman who had not put the money and said

"You did not come here to consult the gods, so the gods have nothing to tell you."

He switched over to the client he had now identified, placed the rattle on her left ear for about a minute and then announced.

"You are lucky that your situation shall be looked into. It will not cost quite much so don't be worried."

He had noticed that the woman was certainly not poor.

"You will come back tomorrow, but alone." he said and could not help looking longingly at the bed.

"You will come with a very big cock. The gods do not accept the cock of the white man though. It must be a cock that can crow and make hens happy."

"I have heard" she replied. Anything else."

"You will also bring along the sum of two hundred thousand francs"

Funyah watched closely whether she would protest. He always charged high, and then had a clever way of bringing down the price if he discovered that his client was not capable. It seemed to be OK with her, so he continued.

"Don't forget Kola nuts too, and a bottle of whiskey good whiskey, not the lousy stuff from Nigeria."

When he noticed that the woman still accepted without hesitation he added.

"You may bring a bonus amount to further please the gods and make them work hard on your problem."

"How much?" she asked without hesitation.

The crook smiled "It depends on you. Any amount that you can afford, but it should be substantial. It could even go up to another two hundred thousands and the gods will immediately rise to their task."

"Tomorrow then." said the lady standing up. "Odeli lets go." she said to the other female.

As the women were moving down to their vehicle, they were marvelling at Funyah's powers.

"And despite the fact that there were two of us, he could still make out that you were the one who had come to consult." Odeli said to her sister.

"I am lucky, I came to the right place." replied Bih.

The next day Bih came back with a sizable cock and the money. She was clumsily clutching a bottle of expensive whisky with her handbag and the cock as she went up to Funyah's shrine.

Funyah received her outside and led her into the shrine. He had a satisfied smile on his face and was prepared to extract as much as possible from this naïve woman.

"Sit on that stool." he told her, lowering his squat bulk to the carpet.

"Give me the cock and the whiskey." he ordered.

She handed over the items and opened her handbag from which she took out the money. Funyah collected the money and counted. It was three hundred thousands francs.

"Good." he said smiling.

This meant that the woman was quite rich and if handled carefully, he would be able to milk her well. He turned and placed all the items among the frightful shrine idols that passed for gods, shook his rattle and listened.

"The gods have accepted your offerings." he declared "Rest assured, everything will be fine."

Funyah rubbed the bald pate on his head and smiled.

"I have been communicating with the gods, and they have told me everything about you and your problem and perhaps more."

"That is wonderful." she replied "So you know why I came already?"

"Everything." replied Funyah. "I know everything about you and why you have come. However, our procedure here is that the gods help you only when you have spoken out your problems to them yourself.

I am here to help you if you forget something, since I know everything."

"So I tell the gods my problems?" asked Bih.

"Yes! Just turn and face the shrine and say out everything. Don't forget that my role is only to remind you about anything that you might have forgotten."

"But why do I need to tell them what they are supposed to know already?" Bih asked.

"Are you a Christian?" Funyah asked.

"Of course!" Bih replied.

"Your Christian God is supposed to know everything, yet you still pray to him for things. At times you even call on others to intercede on your behalf. It is the same here. Although the gods know everything, you have to tell them yourself and it is only then that I can intercede on our behalf.

Bih turned towards the shrine. She was still marvelled about the powers of Funyah and his gods. Imagine knowing everything about her when they had never met, apart from her yesterday's visit. She folded her hands and started.

"I came here because…"

"No!" interjected Funyah. "Although the gods know everything about you, you start by telling them your names. Remember that they work directly on your request which means that you must tell them everything all over."

"My name is Bih" said the lady "My husband is a former minister and up till now we don't know why such a hardworking and fair person was thrown out and why up till now he has not been recalled into another portfolio."

Funyah immediately saw his chance. He was certain that the former minister in question was the bloke who had come to him about one month ago to get him to work for his reappointment, and he had given him the difficult task of sleeping with his daughter. He had assumed that the fool would come back, pleading that the task was impossible, thus making it possible to extract more money under the pretext that he was preparing an alternative solution. The fellow's name was Nikang and this was his wife, no doubt. The fellow had not come back since and Funyah was already getting worried that he might have scared him off with that virtually impossible demand.

"I said everything should be complete." he told her. "You should have started by completing your names. Either you say Bih Nikang or Bih wife of Minister Nikang."

"It is true that you are a powerful man!" she exclaimed. "You knew my name and my husband's name all along from your gods?"

"But I told you so" replied Funyah proudly. "Now go on and don't leave anything out."

"I am Bih, wife of Nikang, the ex minister of Tourism. My husband was dropped from his post five years ago and we

132

don't know why. He is such an honest and hardworking man. Since he lost his portfolio, he has remained faithful to the regime and the party. But then, appointments come and go and he is left in the cold."

"That is good." said Funyah. "You have recounted just what the gods told me. Now they also told me the request you have to make. Say it to them."

"Gods of this great man, Funyah, I want you to help my husband. Let him be given another ministerial post so that we regain our past glory and honour."

Funyah had heard enough on which to work. He put up his hands for her to stop. Shook his rattle a few times, sat quiet for about three minutes, pretending to be communicating with the gods, then declared.

"The gods had already prepared a solution to your problem. Now that you have made a formal request yourself, they will see what to do. You see, your husband's case is not unique. Most of the former ministers who have been recalled passed through here. They come from all over.

This is your special effort, not so?"

Bih nodded "My husband knows nothing about my coming here."

"Keep it that way." said Funyah "Don't say anything to him about this. It is the wish of the gods."

Funyah shook his rattle again, listened for a while and declared.

"The gods have spoken. Your husband's case is pretty bad. There are jealous family members and friends who have blocked him from prospering, whereas he has great prospects. He could even become prime minister. We have to release him from their wicked spell, and then work for his reappointment and progress. You will bring the penis of an albino and the heart of a dwarf child. These are the items needed."

As Bih gasped in horror, Funyah said, "This even is small. Another ex minister from Douala was here the other day and the oracle asked him to sleep with his own daughter apart from other things."

"Why would the gods go to such extremes?" she asked.

"You are asking for so much, so you must pay well for what you ask" replied Funyah.

"Thank God my girls are all out of the country" she said. "My husband is so ambitious and eager to be reappointed. He could end up here also and be asked to sleep with his own daughter."

"What the gods ask from you is different from the other person." replied Funyah. "Besides, this other parliamentarian was from Douala"

Funyah was doing everything to ensure that the woman in front of him should remain ignorant of the fact that her husband had been there first and was indeed the person who had been asked to sleep with his own daughter.

"Please," she said. "Plead with the gods on my behalf. What they are asking for is impossible. Where do I get the penis of an albino? Where would I have the heart to murder a dwarf child and extract the heart?"

"You have money" replied Funyah. "You could easily pay a few thugs to do that for you. I will give you a whole week for that. Don't forget that once the gods are consulted, their appetite is awakened and they don't like to wait long."

"Then, I might just have to give up the whole thing" she said.

"You cant" replied Funyah. Once their throats are tickled, the gods must be satisfied otherwise they will turn on you."

"Is there no way out?" she asked in desperation.

"Only one." replied Funyah "But go and try to fulfil their request first. If you find it completely impossible, come back and we try that one way out."

She was quite shaken as she came out from Funyah's lair and moved down to where she had packed her car. Odeli was waiting inside and her heart quickened as she observed the countenance on her sister's face.

"What happened?" she asked in alarm.

"The gods!" she said simply.

"Gods? Have they refused to do the work?"

"Not really, but their demands are unrealistic."

"What do they want? I thought the large sum of money requested was enough."

"They have asked for more. They want the penis of an albino and the heart of a dwarf child. To get these two items I will have to murder an albino male and a dwarf child. Can you imagine that?"

"That is impossible" said Odeli.

"What do I do?" lamented Bih "And I do so want my husband to get reappointed. We are already losing all the respect we had."

"I have always distrusted these traditional witch doctors." said Odeli. "I am sure the problem is that your husband does not pray hard enough. You need deep prayers and meditation. I could help you there."

"What prayers?" shouted Bih "We go to church every day, contribute generously to the church and even belong to church associations."

"Perhaps, but that is not enough." declared Odeli "What you are doing is barely enough as routine thanks to God for your life, your children and the things you have had so far. Remember your husband was a minister. Now that you want something special, add special prayers. Apart from going to

135

church every morning, pray together every night before you sleep, and please pray sincerely and concentratedly."

"Are you sure mere prayers can enable my husband to be reappointed?" asked Bih "I believe some extra force is required. You really believe that mere prayers without some extra force could help?"

"There you go." said Odeli "You don't term prayers, 'mere.' Prayers are everything. Jesus prayed often and prayers have been known to work wonders. God will help you without asking you to do such wicked things like what that wizard is asking you to do. The highest he would ask you, could be to shave your hair and wear sack cloth."

"Anyway the witch doctor said there is one way out. I think I will go for that one. I only hope it is not as horrid as what has been asked by the gods."

Funyah was relaxing happily on the bed in his shrine. He had good whisky and money, with the prospect of having more. He was sure the foolish woman would not have the heart to go knocking down albinos and dwarf children for the body parts he had requested. She would certainly come back for that last option and that is when he would sample her sumptuous buttocks. At that time too, she would be prepared to give up even a million francs.

He climbed down from the bed, poured himself a glass of whiskey and took a large gulp. He enjoyed the burning sensation and warm glow as the liquid went down his throat into his stomach.

At that same moment, honourable Nikang was relaxing in his house drinking wine and reflecting very hard. He had successfully had sex with his daughter as requested by the medicine man and was supposed to report back to Funyah to solidify his chances of getting reappointed. He was quite sure nobody had suspected that the rape of his daughter had been arranged, apart from that nice neighbour who had finally understood his plight. The thieves had been well paid so they would never reveal anything. But what if they decided to blackmail him? No. he was not sure those boys were up to that. By the time they finished the money, he had given them, he would be far away in Yaounde and an untouchable minister. He had to go back to the witch doctor soon.

Bih had reflected over the advice of her sister Odeli, but decided that prayers alone would not work wonders. She had considered hiring a few thugs to bring her the body parts and had even made contact, but the amount of money they had charged for the job was far beyond what she could muster in a hurry. She had then decided on the last option that Funyah would propose. She finally went back to Funyah alone. She parked at the usual spot and went up on foot. Funyah was waiting for her outside as usual and led her in, smiling satisfactorily. He was certain that she had not succeeded in getting the penis of an albino and the heart of a dwarf child.

When they sat down, he asked.

"Have you brought the items the gods asked for?"

"It was not possible" she replied "Why did the gods not ask for body parts from ordinary people?"

"One can never quite understand the ways of the gods" replied Funyah "Even us, their oracles."

"I think we should try that last option of yours, whatever it is." she said.

"Its quite simple" replied Funyah "It involves cash and sex."

"What do you mean?" Bih said, alarmed.

"You will offer sex to the gods, through me as their oracle of course." Funyah said, maintaining a straight face.

"But gods cannot be interested in things like sex", she said in consternation.

"It is only the Christian God that is said to be chaste." replied Funyah "Gods have always been known to require sex. Pagan gods in the bible, Greek and Roman gods were always involved in sex. I read a bit you know. I am not like those ignorant charlatans that have never been to school and know only a few herbs. I am quite developed and even use the signs of the Zodiac. Look there on the far wall."

"Okay" she said. "I suggest we skip the sex and I double the money."

"That cannot work!" replied the determined Funyah. "Here, we do everything the gods ask us to do. It is not within our powers to change anything. Besides I have not even told you how much money the gods have asked for."

"How much is it?" she asked going for the handbag.

"Not so fast." said Funyah. First, you offer sex to the gods. The amount to be paid will be determined by how well you satisfy them. If they are sexually satisfied and contented, then the cash payment will certainly be low."

Bih sat for about ten minutes confused. She was not a frivolous woman and had rarely had the urge to cheat on her husband. She had been tempted a few times no doubt by handsome bucks but had succeeded in standing her grounds. Here she was, faced with the repugnant prospect of sleeping with a squat ugly medicine man. His cloths were clean and it looked like he had a bath everyday, but he was still very unattractive. At the same time, she was cornered, although she had to admit that the lecher was of a different class, not the usual sordid Sooth Sayer with rotten teeth, badly stained by Kola nuts and bad breath.

"Okay" she said "Let's get over with it quickly. She stood up and started undressing. In excitement Funyah pushed the door close with his left foot and dragged her to the bed. He was afraid that she might change her mind.

After another sip of the expensive wine from the glass he was holding, Nikang checked his pocket with the other hand to make sure he had taken the money destined for Funyah. It had been more than a month since he had been given the task of sleeping with his daughter. Since he had finally succeeded in doing that, he was now in a hurry to round up with the whole thing. He picked up his car keys and went out. Madam had gone out with the other vehicle and this pleased him because he did not have to tell anybody where he was going. He drove to Funyah's and was surprised to see his wife's car well parked. He had never imagined his wife consulting witch doctors. She was such a fervent Christian and often obliged him to pray more than his quota. He moved up the path to Funyah's lair.

In his hurry to have his coveted price, Funyah had dropped his phone and it had switched off as it bounced off a stone. The look out man was sweating as all his calls to alert Funyah of another visitor were not going through.

Oblivious of what was happening; Nikang moved up to the shrine and was surprised that Funyah was not waiting for him outside. As he stood there confused, he thought he heard grunts of pleasure from inside. In an attempt to establish the amount of money that would be demanded by the gods to the barest minimum, Bih was giving her best.

Nikang almost turned to leave, but remembered that his wife's vehicle was parked out there and from every indication some love act was going on inside the shrine. He even thought he heard her gasping with pleasure. He turned the door knob and discovered that it was not locked. He pushed it open and stepped in. for a full minute he could not believe his eyes. Then Bih jumped up from the bed struggling to cover herself.

Nikang could stand it no longer. He dropped to the ground like a log as his heart stopped beating.